To KEEP the SUN RISING

MIRANDA LENWEST

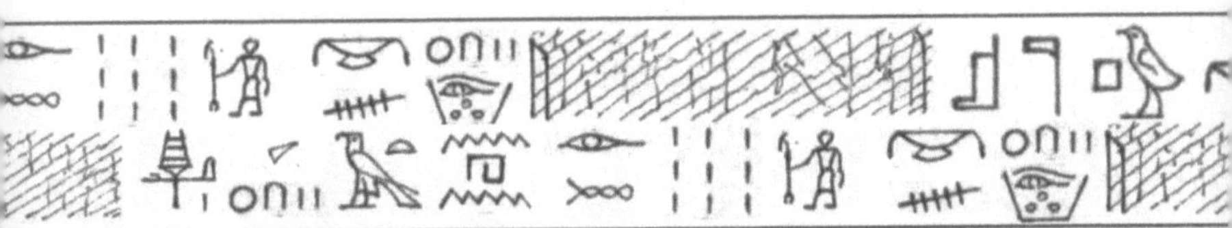

3

To my husband Adam:
I'm yours until the sun no longer rises

FOREWORD

No AI was used in the writing or editing of this novel. I do my best to do due diligence to ensure everyone I work with also doesn't use AI. I believe art needs a human soul.

To Keep The Sun Rising does not contain explicit content - there is no graphic violence, language, or sexual content.

However, I have the utmost respect for the desire to know if certain topics are in a book that you may want to avoid for whatever reason. With that in mind, you can see anything I would consider a content warning on my website at:

www.mirandalenwest.com/to-keep-the-sun-rising

TABLE OF CONTENTS

1
SOLSTICE

The rising of the sun was always a certainty for mortals. They did not question whether it would take place; it simply *happened,* and a new day began. Humanity was blissfully unaware that for many years their next morning was not assured.

I had a complicated relationship with this reality. The sole reason I existed was to serve and protect my father, Ra, the ancient god of the sun. Without that, I had no purpose.

But that wasn't all. The god of chaos, Apep, wanted to stop our efforts. If he succeeded, the sky would turn red and then the world would fall into an eternal night. But that is just what mortals would see. The real threat would be all the power that darkness would provide for him.

Thus, the trajectory of my life revolved around making sure that each night, we kept evil at bay and our people saw another sunrise. And every time it did? I fell into a forced sleep.

But the Summer Solstice was different. It was the day I enjoyed the fruits of my labor, a break from my normal duties thanks to the length of time the sun shone. No matter how I felt about the efforts I went through to protect it, I couldn't deny the warmth I felt when it hit my skin.

"Bastet, are you ready to go?" my sister asked, tapping her foot impatiently.

I had been standing outside our father's temple for a while, basking in the desert's morning sunlight. I did this every time I got the chance, which was rare. Once my duties alongside my father concluded, little time remained before sleep.

"You really don't enjoy this at all?" I questioned, getting up from the outer wall of the temple I had been leaning against.

Sekhmet shrugged. "I suppose I can vaguely recognize the appeal. But I would get way less done if I walked around in this—so many mortals awake and watching. I prefer being able to see when my enemies can't, anyway."

She also belonged to the night, as it was the time she hunted criminals and those who threatened our father's rule. We were *both* born to help fill in the gaps created by Ra having to spend each night protecting the sun.

"And after all, 'cats thrive in the night', right?" I teased.

It was the mantra our father had been telling us since we were old enough to ask questions. And yes, he had chosen us to be feline deities for a reason. Having a body mostly resembling a human but with the head and associated benefits of a cat set us up for success. The nocturnal proclivities, better sight at night, and nimble movements made the most sense for our respective duties.

My sister's head resembled a fierce, golden leopard. I liked to tell myself mine looked like a panther, but most would say it matched the cats mortals kept as pets. My understanding was that those domestic cats, however, did not just thrive at night—they also enjoyed the sun.

My father's temple, like all those of the major gods of Egypt, existed in Heliopolis. Both deities and mortals shared the city, though the latter did not know their city had different levels.

If a mortal looked up, the celestial sphere would obscure their view of the sky. We could look down at them whenever we liked, but they could not look up and see us. We called it a sphere because that was the shape of the magical force-field that obscured their view.

This godly realm as a whole was separate from theirs, accessible only by magic portals that allowed those with holy power to enter. To humans, these portals appeared in various forms —doors that opened to nothing, or red granite pillars called *obelisks* that seemed decorative.

The celestial festival grounds directly mirrored the mortal one. Festivals in Heliopolis happened outside a grand pyramid, in a fenced-off area paved in limestone. The space was full of special religious altars and stages for performers, all set up in front of the Nile River.

Ours just happened to be a little more opulent.

Like theirs, the path to the Festival Grounds of the gods was paved in limestone, though I preferred to walk in the desert sand and feel it between my toes. On festival days, I wore my nicest golden sandals.

We both wore our festival attire, composed of long, flowing white dresses featuring gold trim, in a V-neck cut to highlight our matching sun amulets. I loved watching mine sparkle in the light.

While I continued to enjoy our walk and the light summer breeze, Sekhmet kept worrying about more practical matters. "I hope the offerings are good this year," she said, looking below over the edge of the sphere at the people gathered at the mortal festival.

"One of our only days of real freedom, and what's you're worried about?"

"The rise of the Nile isn't just an excuse to throw a party, sister," Sekhmet remarked with a glare. "As you are well aware, the results of the previous year's harvest—the offerings the mortals bring—determine what blessings I can provide this upcoming season. So yes, that is my primary concern."

The comment stung a bit, but only because I realized I hadn't been considerate of my people at all. I didn't get to spend time with them or answer their prayers the same way my sister did. Her duties took her into the city, letting her interact with her followers. I spent all the time with my father in the underworld, doing my protective duties.

Mortals respected the Nile River the same as they did any deity. Because it did not rain often, it served as our most important water source. The strength of its water affected the crops grown by humans. The solstice festivities included the release of the Nile waters to kick off the start of a new agricultural season.

The luxury of our festival grounds came into view as we walked up to the golden arch that served as an entrance. Grand sandstone columns carved with hieroglyphs that told stories predating my existence by centuries surrounded the area.

"My favorite sisters!" Our brother Shu rode in on a light gust of air, grinning. While he did not possess an animal head like us, he was unquestionably a god. For one, anyone could see his powers over wind always on display. The bird feather peeking out of his black hair kept flapping even once he had stopped in front of us.

"That's not how that works…you can't have more than one favorite," Sekhmet noted, rolling her eyes.

"Well, you can't make me choose, so don't try!" Shu put his hand to his forehead as if the idea stressed him out. It was not just his powers that paid homage to the wind—his voice was airy and light, and his blue eyes glittered like the sky.

I laughed. "Is everyone else here?" Father had left a while ago, as the host of the Solstice Festival. The Summer Solstice strengthened his power, since it was the longest day of the year.

"Most of the key players, but Father won't start the feast until everyone gets here, of course."

The scent of the food wafted in from behind him. I smelled vegetables spiced with cumin, fresh bread, and a savory mix of different meats, some in stews and others served on their own. Like sleep, food was useful to regain energy and strengthened our magic. It was not a necessity in the same way it was for mortals, but it was certainly a welcome boost. Most of us still ate multiple meals a day like they did, but it was useful not to have to if traveling or in a precarious position.

"Sister, you should really take this opportunity to socialize with some new deities," my brother continued, likely seeing me already eyeing my normal table in the back. His voice was still light, but less joking.

Among fellow deities, the hierarchies were more tenuous. Amun started all creation and therefore reigned as the perpetual king of gods. He commanded immense power. No one could guess its full limits, if it had any. Ancient gods had both a large flow of magic and time on their side.

When decisions needed to be made for the good of Heliopolis, it was the ancient gods who gathered to meet. Occasionally, trusted advisors and favorites received invites. Amun certainly played favorites, and my father was one of those. Many viewed him as second in command.

I had the potential to enter adulthood with a decent level of prestige because of my father. Someone who cared about such things would likely follow my brother's advice to socialize with the right gods. But I did not.

Sekhmet had always been better at that game than I, her reputation garnering respect because of her work in Lower Egypt. Shu always encouraged me to "make connections" so that one day I could naturally fit within the major gods and be taken seriously like her.

But I'd never been good at that. I had such limited time in a day to spend time with anyone outside of the underworld. I'd rather spend it with people I liked than try to impress strangers.

"Sure, sure," I replied with a wave of the hand to his suggestion. "Next time, for certain."

Shu sighed. "Sister, you are almost of age; there are only so many next times…"

"I will take your words to heart," I assured him as I walked away, though we both knew I didn't mean it.

"Until later," Sekhmet said, bidding us farewell as she went to her regular spot at a table off to the side with other war gods.

"Alright, enjoy the festivities," Shu relented.

Not wanting to give him the chance to change his mind, I quickly found the familiar walnut table.

"And I was starting to wonder if the feast would start without you," my friend Ptah teased, standing as I approached, towering over me by almost a foot. Like my brother, he could *almost* pass as mortal, if not for the golden sheen over his dark skin.

"As if I'd ever miss the rise of the Nile?" I teased back, reaching out my arms.

His *yusek* (an ornamental golden collar) pressed into my skin as he gave me a quick hug. He hadn't updated the rest of his wardrobe, donning his white linen tunic and the usual blue head covering with the gold trim that concealed most of his hair.

"Is that a trimmed beard?" I asked, noticing it was shorter.

He ran his fingers through it. "Yes, it was your idea, if you remember…do you like it?"

"I'm just impressed you listened to me. I haven't seen you cut that thing since you grew it…"

I was distracted by a pair of eyes watching me. A frog-half-god stared at me from a nearby table. His face was not familiar, but he potentially recognized me as one of Ra's children. When I met his gaze, he quickly looked away and fidgeted in his seat. *Perhaps it's his first public event,* I thought.

I recognized some faces at our table as we sat down. To my left sat Wadjet, the cobra goddess. Her powers were major enough that she would likely be welcome at other tables, but she worked as one of the prominent half-god mentors—connecting them to pharaohs whom they would watch over.

It was not a popular position to take on. Half-gods were the offspring of mortals and gods, something Amun clearly disapproved of by providing them with limited powers and weaker strength. If claimed by their divine parent, they had a chance at gaining good status, but did not happen often. This made them the source of frequent rumors.

Elsewhere at the table, Hatemehit gave me a little wave. I did not really understand her fish powers, but she was always nice to me, so I liked her anyway. She also didn't judge me for eating, which was a pleasant bonus.

"Good to see you," I greeted Wadjet and Hatemehit as I sat down.

It was tempting to dive right into the food piled on the porcelain plates at the center of the table. A chicken dish covered in a creamy sauce that smelled of lemon particularly enticed me. But we weren't supposed to eat anything other than fruit before the feast started. I poured myself a glass of wine.

I turned to Wadjet. "How are the relations with the Pharaohs?"

She took a sip of her own drink. "The world of human politics is certainly never boring. Their lives are short, their minds work so differently…"

I nodded, though I didn't truly understand. "You must spend more time with them than with the rest of us combined." I felt a twinge of jealousy. I'd never even spoken to a mortal still on the plane of the living.

"I will tell you this—they are certainly loving the new pyramid Ptah designed." She lifted her goblet in his direction.

Ptah shrugged, looking away from the table with a slight smile. "It's nothing too impressive."

"If it's anything like the waterfall I saw him design the other week, I'm certain it is," I insisted.

"Does it seem like we are starting even later this year?" he asked, changing the subject.

"It does seem like a servant has brought at least three servings of bread," Wadjet remarked.

I noticed people whispering and looking around. "Well, they should be used to the fact my father will not start until Knum arrives, so I'm not sure why they are surprised. We can't kick off the festival without him." The ancient ram god did not value punctuality.

I felt eyes on me. The frog half-god was watching me again and fidgeting with something in his hands.

"Who is that?" I asked Wadjet, gesturing in his direction. "Is he one of your mentees?"

She looked up. "The frog god? I just met him today…" Before she finished, he was walking toward us. As he grew closer, I noticed his frog head was larger than the rest of his body, as if he hadn't quite grown into it yet.

"Bastet?" he blurted out.

"Yes, that's me…"

"I was uh- given this…message to give to you." He held out a small sealed letter, his hand trembling a bit.

I sighed. "If this is a matter for the court of Ra, he will have an audience next—" I was not a conduit for my father, despite what many people seemed to assume.

"I—I haven't read it or anything," he said, croaking nervously. "Someone just paid me some gold, and I honestly need it…"

In that moment, his human side showed. Mortals and their money, I would never understand it. Gods used it to purchase luxuries, but we did not need it. I wouldn't want to be beholden to it.

I looked around to check for watching eyes, grateful for the sounds of clinking glasses and the chatter holding people's attention. I bit my lip as I pulled open the envelope with little trouble; my mouth suddenly went dry.

The print inside was barely legible.

Dear Bastet,

My name is Tawaret. I am the former wife of the god of chaos. And I need to speak with you. I will wait for you at your temple.

2
FEAST

My mind started to spin. Former wife? Divorce was forbidden among the Egyptian gods. I tried to remember the stories my father had told me about Apep's banishment to the dark. Had she not gone with him?

I stretched out my fingers to keep them steady.

"Who gave you this?" I demanded of the half-god, who still stood in front of me, shifting his weight from side to side. I looked him up and down, but he wore no jewelry or markings that showed a clear alliance to any higher deity.

"I don't know; it was a snake goddess or something…but she had this hood on, and I couldn't really see her—" He stumbled over his words.

I wished Sekhmet were with me at that moment. Intimidation was more her forte.

"I will find out either way, by telling me you'll simply prove you aren't to blame," I bluffed.

He started blinking rapidly. "I'd tell you, really I would—"

I shooed him away in frustration. "You have done your duty. Be off. But you may well hear from me again." My mind was racing, and I couldn't exactly interrogate him in front of a crowd.

"Is there trouble?" Ptah whispered as the half-god slowly walked away. Hatemehit and Wadjet were talking to one another, and though surely they noticed the exchange, I appreciated their respect for my privacy.

I shook my head, lowering my volume to match his. "Not here. Later. We need to go to my temple."

Before he had the chance to respond, my father stood up, and an immediate hush fell over the crowd. He presented in his falcon form, which he commonly used for public appearances. Like several of the ancient gods, he could change between a variety of animal heads at will. His golden crown, with a sun at its helm, sparkled in the light.

"My fellow gods of Egypt, I want to thank you, as always, for coming together on this day in which we celebrate the longest day of the sun, and with it, the rising of the Nile for the coming year. I am honored, as always, to be your host."

In response, the audience clapped and clinked their glasses. All the tables were full—my father was one of the few gods who encouraged such an attendance.

"It is because of the work of all those present today that the mortals are loyal to us. By answering their prayers, we show them that we are listening, and in return, they bring us the sacrifices we need for the coming year."

While what he said was true, my father would have no trouble getting offerings on his own.

Although humans remained unaware of the sun's precarious safety, they at least appreciated its existence. It grew their plants and sustained their life.

And my father's popularity? It rubbed off on the other gods who attended—gods who were unlikely to garner enough worshipers on their own to host a successful festival.

Bored by a speech that I had listened to many times before, I let my mind wander.

As a child, I used to daydream about my own festival. If I closed my eyes, I could see it: mortals coming from all over, decked out in panther masks and elaborate dresses. They would bring their domestic cats alongside them, adorned in gold finery. I would bless both under the light of the midday sun, when it was at its highest in the sky.

My whole family would be there, of course, but I would be the one standing up in the front, giving a toast.

I once told Sekhmet about this. She rolled her eyes and said having her own festival sounded like a "hassle", and that she was "just fine getting sacrifices at other people's festivals, like most gods." But she admitted to me she wouldn't mind having to share with fewer deities. I didn't tell her, but I speculated she could host a fabulous party.

The clatter of a dropped fork jolted me back into the present.

"This has always been an important day because of those offerings—but I also have a personal reason to be attached to this day, as it represents the time when my family is all together." My father gestured toward his children.

Shu smiled, I gave the same awkward wave I always did, and Sekhmet gave a curt nod.

He then turned and smiled at the female deity next to him. "I hope one day this family will grow." How had I not noticed that his romantic companion, Hathor, was seated at his right-hand side?

The solar goddess looked undeniably beautiful. She had access to an animal head form, but a cow was perhaps not the most conventionally attractive creature to emulate. So, she did not. She usually presented herself simply as a woman with well-defined curves and enchanting golden eyes.

It was no secret that my father had taken a lover since my mother's passing nearly ten years ago. But she was not even an official consort. Was her position this year meant to imply otherwise?

I glanced over at my sister as my father closed out his opening greeting. "May the solstice begin!" But she sat too far away for me to read her face.

The gods clapped louder this time, and the performers played music. Tefnut, my brother's wife, came forward. She served as the goddess of moisture, marking her a perfect partner for the god of the sky. Together with my father, they sent down a rainbow, a sign that we were ready for offerings. You could faintly hear clapping from the crowd below as well. The festival had officially begun.

As the gods feasted, the people below lined up and offered their crops, wine, and raw materials in piles before the idols of their chosen gods.

Once they had placed their gifts, Khnum stood up and looked over the bounty. Deeming it worthy, he released the water from the caverns to flood the Nile.

Although I had seen it many times, the sound of the rushing waters always impressed me. After some more applause, both above and below, the gods accepted their individual offerings. Like Khnum, they would review the sacrifices to decide their quality and then send down a modest sign of approval, such as making their idol glow.

I never paid much attention during this part —I received no direct offerings myself. I had no time to interact with the public. I wished I did. Still, I sometimes caught my name in prayers or a passing mention in offerings to my siblings or father. People had heard of me and that one day I would step into full godhood. They understood I would be someone of note someday, but not today.

My role alongside my father made me basically invisible. All of my time and the entirety of my divine powers were spent on the journey.

My mind wandered again to the daydream of my imagined festival. In this hypothetical feast, I had more than enough power to go around. I blessed everyone present and stood tall to the sound of clapping.

The power of a god was confined to our life force, otherwise referred to as *ka* levels. Anything we did used *ka,* as simple as using my nocturnal cat sights. A god's *ka level* was determined by many things—our age, lineage, even the domain we oversaw. Amun had determined that some requests should consume more *ka* than others.

These limitations existed to prevent gods from using their powers irresponsibly—not that they stopped some.

But even my daydreams could not distract me from the note in my pocket. I kept fidgeting with it, as if my hands could find new meaning simply by feeling the ink on the page. *Was this message actually from her? What did she want?*

Ptah gently tapped my shoulder. "Would you like us to take our leave?"

I nodded, grateful for the suggestion. We gave a few cursory goodbyes to the others at the table and prepared to exit. Most deities would stay past the setting of the sun; their free time was not as limited as mine. Half-gods would eventually tire, but they pushed themselves as the opportunities to socialize with the major gods were rare.

Shu gave me a look of disapproval, but he did not get up. I was glad. The last thing I wanted was another speech about how I was "wasting valuable opportunities" to talk to gods of high status—let alone having to explain the actual reason I was leaving early.

Once we were on the path back into Heliopolis, Ptah turned to me. "What does the note say?"

"I'll just let you read it," I replied, handing him the letter.

He took only a moment to scan it. "Are you sure this isn't some kind of trap? I don't feel good about this, Bastet. Perhaps we should go back and get your father, or at least your brother…"

I shook my head. "I'm sure it's nothing serious. I wouldn't want to bother them."

It felt easier to lie than explain the strange force I felt toward the invisible writer of the note. That half-god had said the message was for *me*—not the court of **Ra**. I wasn't used to people wanting to meet with me.

Plus, it was *my* temple, not hers. There were wards and protections everywhere. That wouldn't be the best place to set a trap, surely?

I loved my temple. It was one of the first that Ptah had created once he discovered his powers extended beyond shaping rivers, caves, and mountains. It was how we met.

Even back then, although I was quite young, my father could tell I grew weary of my duties. I did not complain in his presence, but I asked a lot of questions about what my powers would be when I was free and what domain I would rule over. I wished I could spend more time reading or doing art instead of riding through the underworld. He could tell I yearned for that day.

Bubastis was made of dark red marble and fine stone. It was not among the largest in the area, but that was not my wish; I simply wanted something that represented my spirit.

For a moment, my heart felt lighter looking at the view from below as we went upstairs. The windows gave a wonderful perspective of the city. It was close enough that I could see mortals walking around, but far enough that the faces were indistinguishable.

"It's so nice to see these columns as the sun shines upon them," I remarked, running my fingers along the cool marble. We walked through the grand entrance, a doorway of impressive size surrounded by two large cat-shaped fountains, whose water flowed back into the nearby rivers.

I clapped lightly when I noticed the multitude of cats in the front throne room. I didn't get to use it, so I had asked Ptah to make it into a cat sanctuary instead, so that people would understand I was preparing a place for them and the creatures I would one day bless more directly. Troughs of food and water lined the floor, and soft linens were carefully sewn into chairs and shelves of various heights along the walls, adorned with my personal inscriptions.

"Thank you," I said, as one of the cats rubbed against my leg.

"Of course," Ptah said, petting a black cat that was meowing for his attention.

Should I ever meet with advisors or priests here, they would simply have to accept their presence.

For now, I had one singular priest. Pawerem mainly cared for the cats and kept up with general upkeep—there wasn't much else to do. My temple wasn't open to the public.

The old man bowed deeply when he saw us approach. "Goddess, I am blessed by your appearance." But he was missing his usual smile.

"There…is someone waiting for you, Bastet."

Now that I stood in my temple, I wished the meeting was happening somewhere else. This was my safe place, a representation of the future I dreamed about. And someone had invaded it.

I didn't blame the priest; I had not given him orders to keep anyone out.

"Yes, could you tell me the location of our er…guest?"

He pointed to a small room off to the side. I did not go in there often as it was mostly a storage space for scrolls. Pawarem kept his logs there about the temple's upkeep, and I had stored some texts on shielding powers that my teachers had given me over the years.

I took a deep breath and walked toward the door, Ptahway following close behind.

"Goddess, I apologize, but she insisted you go in alone."

3

A WARNING

Ptah stepped in front of me as I processed the priest's words. "No, now this definitely seems like a trap, Bast…" he insisted, blocking my path. I could tell he was serious because he was using his nickname for me, the one he only used when showing great concern.

I held up a hand. "Ptah, I appreciate it, I really do. But this is the only door to the room. I promise that if I sense any kind of danger, I will call out, and you can be there in an instant. But I…need to do this."

He frowned but stepped aside. "I'll be listening."

I nodded and went to the door, taking a stabilizing deep breath.

The room inside was dark, with two candles providing light from a table at the center. I could smell the dust, which clung to every surface. I realized I hadn't been here in quite a while, so I quickly scanned the room until I found a window. It was small, but I could probably get out through it if I needed to. As my gaze traveled further, I noticed something else—scales, barely visible.

If it weren't for my night vision, I wouldn't have seen her at all. Tawaret was in full animal form resembling a dark green hippopotamus. She wore an ornamental hood over her face, but her eyes still gleamed through—unmistakably the red of a demon-god.

I shivered. I had never met a demon before. They were not welcome in most divine spaces.

She leaned against a bookshelf but jumped slightly as I closed the door. She did not appear as confident or intimidating as I might have expected a demon to carry themselves.

"You wished to speak?" I asked, forgoing any sort of greeting. I hoped my voice did not betray my nervousness. As she stepped into the candlelight, I kept my distance, hugging the wall.

"You are the daughter of Ra." It was a statement, not a question.

"I am one of them," I responded.

"You are the one who defends Ra as he carries the sun through the underworld against my former…" There was a long pause. "…husband." The word seemed difficult for her to say.

"Correct."

"Then I am speaking to the right daughter… Bastet, I am here to give you a warning." She locked eyes with me. "What has your father told you about his plans to end this conflict?"

"I hardly see how that is a matter I would discuss with you," I snapped, backing up slightly.

I would not reveal the truth to her, that father and I rarely spoke of his plans to slay the chaos god.

"Have I touched a nerve?" Tawaret remarked.

"You of all beings should realize how complicated an endeavor this is. Apep is in the underworld; my father's powers rely on the charge of the light. It is not a simple fight."

"But...he's never asked you to help?" She leaned forward.

Until I reached my full godhood, my strength was little more than that of a half-god. I had my feline senses and a shield ability, which helped me generate a small force-field to ward off basic attacks.

This was the extent of Amun's intervention. He felt responsible for creating Apep, viewing his rebellion as his own failure. But he also told my father "that the world needs darkness as much as it needs light—to facilitate the existence of the moon, to empower the stars to shine."

And so he didn't destroy him. He didn't protect us from the curse.

"That's not...possible yet." I crossed my arms. "But he's working on it. My father will stop at nothing to free us."

He told us that all the time. Sekhmet was patient and didn't ask as often as I did. But I'd never been good at hiding my emotions, so he would offer me reassurances. But they did not include details.

Tawaret raised an eyebrow. "Whatever he has told you, it is not the full story."

"And you believe this...because?"

"Because I only recently learned the truth. I didn't want to come here." Her voice was weary.

"Do you think it was easy approaching you this way? I was unfamiliar with the celestial sphere, so I wasn't sure how else to locate you. I have put myself at great risk."

'Great risk,' I thought bitterly. *Meeting me alone in a sealed temple?* She acted as though she were doing me a favor.

"If it's all such a risk, why not send it by messenger bird? Or through that poor half-god you took advantage of? You didn't need to meet me at all."

She shook her head. "Trust me, I tried. Your father's sentries don't allow messages from someone like me to reach the sun god's daughter."

I frowned. "Are you implying my father censors my mail?" My jaw tightened. *What would father say if he saw me here, entertaining this?*

Tawaret sighed. "I'm not *implying* anything. I'm *telling* you why I had to show up in person when I'd rather not show my face. Which is what you asked me. I couldn't wait any longer."

"Why not?" I demanded.

"It's almost—" She hesitated, furrowing her brow. "It will make sense once you hear the prophecy…which you must find yourself."

The words made my heart freeze. It took me a moment to respond. "What…prophecy?"

"I can't—" She put a hand over her mouth in frustration. "The— It's not a truth I can offer you, even if you would accept it from me, which I doubt."

She's not wrong. While she was clearly perfectly sober, her words had the rambling quality of a god under the influence of too much wine.

But there was something in her eyes as she covered her mouth, as though she was trying to say more, but physically couldn't.

I pressed my lips together. "Alright then. Who *can* tell me this prophecy, if not you?"

"Ask your father about a certain revelation from Thoth. He will realize what you mean."

Thoth was the god of wisdom. One of the ancient gods, nearly my father's equal in power. He was the recorder of history and keeper of a vast archive in his temple. He and his wife had given mortals the gift of hieroglyphs.

But more than that, he was a prophet. His prophecies shaped the destinies of many gods, and none had ever proven false.

"If you're right about him supposedly censoring my mail," I pointed out sharply, "why would he confirm this revelation at all?"

Tawaret's lips curved up slightly with the hint of a smile.

"The fact you came to that conclusion on your own is proof that I've given you enough to start down this path. That's what I came for. The rest is up to you. You'll just have to choose whom to trust."

She stepped forward, heading for the door. I held up a hand. "Unless you wish to be seen by my rather protective best friend, I'd suggest the window."

She paused, then nodded, turning toward it.

Wait, I am not ready for her to leave!

I called out to her, stalling. "Are you saying I should trust you?" You're the wife of my family's greatest foe. Whose side are you even on?"

"Could I not say the same for you? That you are the daughter of our enemy." Her gaze sharpened. "My side, Bastet, is whichever one keeps me and those I love alive. I'm inviting you to join me." Tawaret lifted herself onto the windowsill.

"And what do you mean by former wife?" I pressed, desperate for more answers as the conversation slipped away.

"Not now. A time will come for us to speak again, but I have already been gone too long." She paused, turning back once. "But, Bastet, don't wait too long. We're running out of time." Then, she was gone.

I emerged to a relieved Ptah and an anxious Pawerem.

After assuring them I was unharmed, I gestured for Ptah to walk me back home. I did not want to discuss the encounter I had just had in front of my priest.

My head spun. As defensive as I had been during that conversation, I hadn't exactly stopped it.

Why?

Perhaps it was that her words stirred some kind of curiosity within me. It had been a long time since I had asked my father about the status of his search for a loophole or any other way to free Sekhmet and me from our obligation.

Since Sekhmet and I were not yet full gods, we still lived within Ra's temple. It made sense. Sekhmet managed the Lower Egyptian soldiers from a war room Father had built for her.

I kept my voice low as we walked through the streets of the celestial sphere. My temple was close to my father's, but he lived on *Ogdoad,* the street where the original ancient gods lived.

All the streets inside the sphere were paved with sandstone, but as you approached *Ogdoad,* there was a noticeable shift. The stone was more worn and a lighter shade of brown. This was not viewed as a sign of poor quality, but of age and respect.

The temples along this street were larger than all the others. It was easy to tell at a glance which one belonged to which god. For example, Nu, the original water deity, had his temple built upon a lake. To enter, you had to pass through a glass arch filled with running water.

My father's temple was, of course, built to celebrate the sun: wide windows everywhere, statues that sparkled in the light, every detail meant to emphasize the beauty of what my father had created.

I always felt a sense of pride that this was my home. It was one of the few temples created by Amun himself during the age of the original gods. As the years passed, he had little time for such matters and firmly retired from temple building once Ptah took over.

But that pride was mixed with a small, persistent resentment when I found myself surrounded by endless depictions of the sun—of what I could never have.

Only the top half of our temples was inside the sphere. That section held the living quarters and the spaces where the gods conducted business, such as my sister's war room. A staircase led to a portal that opened into the temple below, where mortals came to pray. To them, looking up, it appeared the roof was lost in the clouds, too high to see.

We came to a stop now at the main door to the living quarters, nodding to the guards out front. Since golden armor was quite heavy, they wore steel instead. Their colors did not match the rest of the court, but the suns carved into their helmets made it clear who they served.

Ptah had listened intently as I told him of my meeting with Tawaret. He kept his voice low as he replied. "Bastet, this is…I'm really concerned. You do understand what you must do?"

"Yes, there is only one thing I can do," I responded. "It's time to confront my father."

4

DUAT

I personally did not consider Duat a particularly pleasant or unpleasant place. Yes, the underworld was deeply dark, but not the foreboding kind of darkness mortals seemed to imagine. It was lit by the stars of those who had found peace.

I boarded the Mesktet, the small cedar boat that carried me and our crew of five through the murky waters. Its rims were gold, like everything belonging to the court of Ra, and it stood out from other ships with its unusually tall, sickle-shaped bow and stern.

The captain, a river goddess, nodded in my direction. She always impressed me with how she kept her long, thick hair fit neatly under her maritime cap.

"Have you studied the way for tonight?" I teased.

She rolled her eyes. "Last time I checked, goddess, our route hasn't changed."

Speaking with the crew was my primary entertainment on the nightly journey.

I was the closest to Henet, a white pelican goddess around my age. She was an excellent swimmer, with the power to cleanse polluted rivers and spawn fish in even the smallest streams.

"How was the Solstice?" She asked as the crew prepared for takeoff.

I wanted to pour out my thoughts in a long diatribe, but I didn't. We were too close to my father, who would overhear. Instead, I answered lightly, "How could a day off ever be bad?"

She studied me for a moment, as though deciding whether to press. Then she smirked. "I'm sure it could never match up to one of our festivals," she said with a wink.

Henet and her family belonged to Khonsu's court, the moon god's domain. Our courts were not at odds; they simply oversaw different domains within Egypt. Occasionally, joint festivals brought us all together, or they received invites for diplomacy's sake.

"Yes, well, don't tell my father that. He won't let me skip the Solstice. He already says you're a bad influence."

She grinned. "Because I taught you how to have fun."

She was right. Before Henet, I had been more content with my life. As a child, you do not have a concept of what is normal.

When she joined our crew, she introduced me to the outside world. Even her stories of school fascinated me, like foreign tales. She told me about the little dramas with other celestial children and the multitude of subjects she got to learn. Sekhmet and I had only our priest, training us solely for our roles in Ra's court.

Together we grew up, and though the differences between our daily lives increased, our bond remained strong.

My conversation with Tawaret had pushed me toward finally speaking with my father, but the truth was the discontent started to grow the day I met Henet. Every time she told me of some new experience, I felt equal parts of joy for her and jealousy for myself.

Like the waves swelling until Knum released them to flood the Nile, all Tawaret had merely set them free. And now my questions swirled like the wildness of a flooded river.

The truth was sailing through Duat grew quite boring.

Yes, I was always technically "on guard," weapon at my side. Yes, a vague sense of danger lingered at the back of my mind as I scanned the sea.

But in all my years of defending the sun, there had been only a handful of threats.

The encounters followed a similar pattern—a demon would appear, I would raise my shield and brandish my spear, and then the fight would end before it ever truly began. My father was always unfazed and focused on his task. He would give me a cursory "good job," but wouldn't entertain any of my requests for additional combat training.

"You are here to serve as my guard, not fight demons," he always said.

Perhaps Amun sensed my plight, as another unofficial role emerged for me in Duat—that of guiding mortals on their journey to the afterlife.

The first time a human spoke to me, it took me off guard. But it made sense—if I found myself floating on a small wooden boat in unfamiliar waters, unsure of what was to come, I too might reach out to the vessel carrying the sun.

The conversations varied. Some showered me with questions, others sought reassurance with no need for details. Occasionally, I met an older human at peace who simply nodded at me, content and silent. I was glad I was not the one to judge souls. There were a few I saw that seemed capable of true evil.

But I understood it was only a glimpse. Death equalized all; both the virtuous and the wicked came to judgment. My fleeting conversations with them did not define the whole of who they had been.

On this particular night after the solstice, our journey felt routine. It gave me time to mentally prepare myself for a talk with my father.

A heaviness pressed against my chest, and I couldn't seem to shake it. As I stared at the water, I tried to remember the last time we had even spoken about Apep.

I was so lost in thought that I almost missed the young mortal woman floating next to us. She looked only a few years older than me—a blink of an eye to an immortal. *Why is she here so young?* She wore a white dress, its train filled the boat, and her dark hair blended into the night sky.

"Hello, and welcome to Duat," I said softly.

Her face, solemn yet serene, struck me. Something in her expression reminded me of that first woman I had spoken to. There was no fear. "I see," she murmured. "That's what this is…"

"May I ask what brought you here so soon?" It was not an inquiry I typically made, but there was something enthralling about her.

"I suddenly grew very sick," she told me. "I believe someone in my family first contracted the illness, smallpox. But he recovered. I did not."

As many times before, I wished I had some power to heal mortals. But even if I did, only an ancient god could intervene once a human left their mortal plane. Thus I simply said, "I'm sorry."

The girl shook her head. "Oh, please, you do not need to be. I have no fear of judgment. In fact, a part of me...is looking forward to what comes next, I believe it will be peace."

"How, but...you are so young..." I trailed off, confused.

She smiled. "I have someone waiting for me. My love has been there without me for too long. Do not misunderstand, I wouldn't have left my family by choice. But I also thank the gods for the chance to be reunited with him. Peace will come when we are together again."

A love so strong that this young woman was not just content—she was almost excited for death. I could not fathom it. "I wish for you to find peace. I have no say in the matter, but my heart tells me you will be reunited soon."

"And may you also find peace," she replied, before turning forward and closing her eyes, letting the river carry her onward. There was no need for the mortal to steer—a fact that had confused many over the years, but this girl hadn't even questioned it.

No one had ever said anything like that to me before. Mortals sometimes appreciated me for the kind words, but no one had wished me anything. The fact that it came from someone with no power at all made it more touching.

I knew gods could die—I had seen it when my mother passed. But it was rare, we don't die of old age or typical illnesses. Only powerful gods with powerful weapons could kill one another, at great detriment to their own souls.

Because it was rare, I could never truly picture it. I doubted I could ever meet death with such peace. After all, aside from my mother, no one waited for me.

I had never been in love the way she was. When was there time to find a consort? My life was too confined; I barely spent any time with my peers aside from Henet and Ptah. and rarely met new people. I was not even sure I could fathom what romantic love even felt like.

Perhaps more importantly, I wondered how my soul would be judged.

I shook the thoughts away and glanced at my father. Unsurprisingly, he did not even look up, his focus ever fixed on balancing the sun and scanning the darkness.

I had once asked if he ever listened to my guidance with mortals. He had simply answered: "I do not concern myself with the brief lives of mortals. There are other deities for that. But I appreciate that the conversations mean something to you."

We reached the shore at the usual time. I had no clock to track the hours in Duat, but I always saw the time once we emerged. The journey seemed to take the same time every night, leaving me some days with surplus hours, and others mere moments before sleep.

After releasing the sun to its place in the sky, my father and I began the walk to the temple. Not too far away, but a long enough to walk to give us a moment to speak.

With every step, my heart beat faster.

"Father, may I ask you something?" I wanted to approach the topic carefully, not to make accusations that might shut down any sort of conversation.

"Of course," he responded, though he did not slow his pace.

"We have not discussed a longer-term solution to…Apep in quite some time," I intoned.

He stopped in his tracks. I couldn't decipher his expression, but his voice was level as he replied, "Why are you asking this, daughter?"

"I just wondered…if you'd talked to your priests recently. Regarding their research on magic, if it might help us. If they discovered any loopholes… Or anything else?"

There was no hiding the desperation in my words.

He sighed. "You are right, we haven't discussed this in some time."

"Have they found anything? A champion to take him down, perhaps? Or… Have you spoken with Amun lately?" They did not often speak, the head of the Egyptian gods and my father. But as chief of the gods, Amun sometimes met with my father on matters of war or law.

"There have been many duties filling my days," he responded, his voice trailing off, at first defensive, then softer, as if he realized their impact.

It was true, but it didn't stop me from feeling a pang of sadness at his words.

"I know."

He straightened his shoulders. "But please believe me that there is not a day I do not wish for a fuller life for you and your sister." He started walking again.

I followed suit silently, biting back the urge to echo my words sarcastically. "I know that too."

I glanced up at the moon to determine how much time I had left. I could track it as well as any sundial.

I felt the tension in the air, but I would not be the one to break it.

"Has something prompted this?" he asked at last.

I realized I could've shown my hand at this moment and told him everything. But something stopped me. Perhaps I wanted him to come clean; if there was truth to Tawaret's words, he would come clean himself. Or maybe I was just scared of his answer.

"My coming of age." It was an easy lie, for there was some truth behind it. I would soon reach adulthood. Unlike my peers, I would not naturally ascend at that time and grow into my powers. Instead, the stalemate capped me.

"I see," he responded, his eyes fixed ahead.

Does he believe me?

My steps slowed, unwilling to reach the temple too soon. Unless he had training or business for me, he usually left me to my free hours here.

"Surely you understand my desire to reach my potential and serve the people of Egypt," I pressed, trying to find anything to say that would be as convincing as the truth. I was worried he was hiding something big from me.

"Yes, you will make a wonderful goddess if—when the time comes." his eyes flicked away, as if he didn't want me to see his reaction to the slip-up of his words.

I frowned. *Was that just a mistake?* Or did it mean something?

We were finally at the entrance. "I will see what new information I can bring you, Bastet," my father said. "Be patient and believe that my priority is keeping you safe. Soon, we can discuss more." His voice was gentle, but firm.

I searched his face for any sign of deception. But he had recovered his composure from his slip-up a moment ago; his shoulders loosened, and his facial features remained calm.

"Be patient," I echoed. "I will do my best." My voice sounded hollow.

"That's all I could ever ask." He placed a hand on my shoulder lightly before pulling away and walking in the other direction.

5

THE SEARCH BEGINS

My heart raced as I ran up the narrow stairs of the living quarters. Adrenaline coursed through my veins. I needed to *do* something to start my search for answers. My room was the first in the hallway of bedrooms; a practicality for making sure I made it before I fell asleep.

My room was an ode to countless easy distractions. My old lyre sat in the corner, collecting dust, and a set of *senet* dice lay half out of their box on my nightstand, missing a piece. Behind the door sat a basket, only half-woven.

Most of my hobbies faded like a passing cloud, forgotten before I ever mastered them. But I always returned to painting, which one could see in the well-maintained and carefully stored brushes and canvases. Ptah had introduced me to it, a pastime that carried me to different worlds mentally, even if I couldn't physically.

One of the few organized corners of the room was the small table where the servants left my mail.

The gods sent mail through enchanted ibis birds—long-legged creatures with even longer beaks, perfectly suited to carrying messages and even small parchments. The birds were patrons of Thoth's.

I glanced at the small table near the door where the temple staff always placed my mail. It was normal, right? For someone else to bring you your mail? Yet Tawaret's accusation about censorship clung to my mind.

They must be checking them for safety. While difficult, a being could send something cursed through the mail. Plus, mortals would sometimes send hateful messages if their prayers stayed unanswered.

I opened the newest scroll waiting for me.

I recognized the handwriting immediately—it was from Ptah.

How was it speaking with your father? Did he provide any answers?

His message surprised me. Though he had seemed supportive during our walk home, I hadn't expected him to press me for updates…I didn't expect him to be so impatient.

I realized he had never pushed me once all these years—not to speak to my father, or anyone else, for that matter. He had always accepted our friendship and lived in a small window. Was he growing tired of a best friend who couldn't be awake during the day?

I ran my hand across the parchment, testing the folds. Did it seem secure? Did it look as if it had been opened and refolded?

I sighed. There was no seal and no way to tell if it had been tampered with. I had run up here, hoping I would *feel* something once I opened the letter, a certainty that now felt silly.

But it didn't prove that no one censored my letters either. Nothing was going to be that simple.

I wrote back:

I will pass on to you the same message my father gave me—'we must be patient'.

And then it was time to fall asleep.

Tawaret had chosen the worst possible time to upend my life by the seams. Since the Summer Solstice had just happened, the nights were short, and my free time severely limited. That was always the trade-off I made for my day of freedom—days filled with nothing but work and sleep.

It also meant Ptah visited less, though he still wrote. I had asked him to send a letter—sealed in an envelope, unsigned, written with a different parchment type than he normally used. While I waited for this letter, I sat down to dine with Sekhmet.

Our "dinner" had to be eaten at odd times, of course. When the nights were short, we often ate quickly and alone. But today we resumed our shared meal in what we referred to as the guest dining room. Though much smaller than the main dining room, it had a plush design, with finely polished marble tables and paintings featuring various ancient gods.

"Is something troubling you, sister?" Sekhmet asked, setting down her fork. She had just finished the salmon the waitstaff had brought in, while mine sat untouched.

I had had some guilt of course, hiding things from her. But her relationship with our father had always been more militant than mine. Maybe because of her war god roots, but she was a fantastic soldier. She took orders and didn't question them. To confide in her, I would need far more proof.

If I tell her the truth, she'll try to talk me out of it.

I bit my lip. "It's about Father…" I started.

"The fact that he had Hathor seated so close at the Festival?" she leaned forward. "That was quite strange, yes? You don't think he plans to actually wed that *indecent* woman, do you?"

"Sister!" I gasped. "That's an ancient goddess you're talking about."

"In age only," she scoffed. "Her powers are useless, and her cow form hardly inspires confidence."

"She isn't just skilled in music and dance, if that's your implication."

Sekhmet rolled her eyes. "Right, she supposedly has 'sky powers' no one has seen her use in a century. She's not good enough for father, I'm sure you agree; you're just too polite to say it."

It's not that I harbored any fondness for Hathor, but neither did I share Sekhmet's disdain. I had rarely spoken with her. Father had never hidden her from us; in fact, on the contrary, he had actually encouraged us to bond with her over the years. But never pushed, and I had never tried.

Sekhmet's dismissals seemed unnecessarily harsh, so I asked, "Why, because her powers aren't impressive enough for you?"

She raised an eyebrow. "Certainly you've learned her reputation?" When I didn't respond, she leaned in closer. "They say she has two children no one has ever claimed. Whoever their father was, he refused to stand by them."

Realization hit me, and my eyes widened. "She's been married before?"

"Unless they were mortals. I am not sure which one is worse, really. Do you see why we must protect Father from her?"

If it is true, it was certainly a stain against her character. "But how can we protect him? He must be aware of what people say. Why would he listen to us?"

"No," she insisted. "I'm not holding my tongue any longer. If I don't say something soon, he'll move her into our temple!"

She seemed so sure he would take her seriously. It made me a bit jealous, and more importantly, brought me back to my own concerns. If she had been the one to ask about Apep, would he have given her a real answer? I wanted to ask her advice, without telling her about Keket.

"How often do you speak to our father… plainly?" I asked, fiddling with the handkerchief under my plate.

"What do you mean?" Sekhmet tilted her head, all the heat of her comments about Hathor gone, replaced by casual suspicion.

"Well…" I trailed off. "We don't talk as much as you guys do; he is mostly silent in Duat. And then afterwards, he advises on matters of court, right? Like getting…status updates?"

I realized how little I understood my sister's routines. Had she hidden it, or had I never asked?

She sipped her goblet and furrowed her brow. "Yes, something like that…"

"Do you ask him for permission for things, or is it more like…" I paused, searching for the right word. "Getting advice, or a final sign-off?" *Did that even make sense?* I was trying to gauge if he treated her more like an equal.

She set her goblet down. "Well, of course, he trusts my instincts. He spends most nights with you, so I must make a lot of decisions on my own. If something urgent comes up while you guys are gone, I usually ask one of our advisors."

The idea struck me, showing me an angle I hadn't considered. I had never even spoken to an advisor or priest without Father present, except the occasional small talk.

"You meet with them by yourself?" I asked, surprised.

"On occasions, when I need to, yes. He trusts them, so I trust them. Many of the half-gods have served him for decades and can safely guess how he would decide."

I noticed a slight spill on the table and dabbed it away with the handkerchief, my mind racing.

The advisors have knowledge of his plans.

It resembled the click when you finally used the right key on a lock. My father was not working alone. He had people doing research, looking through historical texts, and experimenting with different magical solutions.

Of course, I had gone to him first—out of respect. But he told me to trust my instincts? And right now, they told me I needed answers. He wasn't ready to give them.

When I got back to my room, I picked up a papyrus and a reed pen. I moved slowly, not trusting was doing the right thing. I held it so long in the air that a splotch of ink dripped on the papyrus, causing me to throw it out and start again.

But then the letter from Ptah arrived. I nervously ran my fingers over it, not sure if I wanted to find evidence of tampering or not. At first, everything seemed normal until my fingers felt something odd around the seal. It was so slight, I likely would not have noticed it before. But I saw the tiniest bit of residue—evidence of an altered seal.

I dropped the letter in shock. *She was right!*

Filled with new vigor, I picked up my pen to write a message to my father's priests and advisors, requesting them to meet me as soon as I returned from Duat, without my father.

6

THE COUNCIL

I had always considered the meeting room one of the most beautiful in the temple. It featured enormous windows found throughout the rooms, more than any other. The sight was breathtaking, the rising and setting sun centered perfectly above an enormous pyramid. Once, as a child, I was determined to view the sunrise. Someone moved me to my sleeping quarters after I passed out.

On the opposite wall from the windows stood bookshelves of white marble. It was full of records from previous meetings and, more interestingly, magic scrolls the priests had gathered relevant to Ra's domain. I always sense a kind of connection to them. Even before I could read, I would rub my hands over the embossed ink and stare at the illustrations.

As a god, some kind of magic existed within me. Something beyond the feline gifts our kind shared: the night vision, the nimbleness, a strong affinity toward fighting birds or rodents. But there was likely more, perhaps light magic, or water, or even fire, though the first seemed most likely based on my father.

But I had never been able to pursue it. I trained as a child in defense, to ward off Apep or his followers if they made a move. But true magic belonged to full goddesses, and my sister and I didn't make the cut in our current form.

The table was full. On each side sat four priests and four priestesses respectively, and one half-god and half-goddess. They wore the typical colors of members of Ra's court: whites, golds, and the burnt orange representing the sun's core. They were of varied ages and backgrounds, but unquestionably the best Egypt had to offer.

I did not recognize the half-gods, one with eagle-like features and the other spouting goat-like horns. One of the older priestesses looked familiar. Her red hair was piled into a massive bun and held by a pin featuring an opal gemstone. But I couldn't place how I recognized her.

I paced across the hall to my father's primary office, where he held smaller meetings. The closed door meant he was in a meeting with someone. This made me pause. Protocol dictated that I wait until the meeting ended. But every moment I didn't have answers felt like an eternity.

Stopping made my thoughts spin.

I wouldn't accept anything until I heard it from my father himself. *There has to be some kind of explanation.* My father had a large court…perhaps he had talked to a different group of advisors? Or maybe he was *having* conversations they weren't present for.

I lifted my hand, which I hadn't realized was shaking. Muscle memory compelled me to knock on the door, but I had no intention of asking for permission to enter. Instead, I thrust the door open.

My confidence slipped as I stood in that office, full to the brim with documentation I wasn't allowed to touch. It wasn't like one of our libraries. This room held battle plans, secret intelligence, classified communication, and a part of me wanted to tear them down and hold it for ransom until everything made sense.

My father was meeting with a scorpion god I didn't recognize. They both leaned over a map on my father's desk. The god immediately stood up when I entered, brow furrowed.

"Bastet, has something happened? Surely you would not interrupt an active meeting otherwise, *yes?*" He immediately folded the map they had been studying. *Just another secret, locked away.*

"I just met with your advisors," I declared, straightening my shoulders and holding my head high. "And I want you to tell me the truth." I strode to the desk, meeting my father's eyes.

The scorpion goddess picked up a document and moved to the door. "I...perhaps I should excuse myself." She gave a light bow before excusing herself. It was less than a minute, but it felt like an hour.

I did not make the moment less awkward for my father by not looking at her or apologizing for the interruption.

He did not speak until she closed the door. "You…summoned my advisors to a meeting without me there?" He tipped his head slightly.

I crossed my arms. "It was the only way to get answers."

"What answers?"

I put my hand on the desk, stabilizing myself. "Have you stopped looking for ways to fight Apep?"

He broke our gaze; his shoulders sagged with resignation. He took a deep breath. "Daughter… please sit down."

Why isn't he denying it? Why isn't he telling me the very idea is ridiculous?

"I'd actually rather prefer to stand," I responded, my voice trembling. "Are you saying it's true then?"

"Bastet, there is so much you have not heard. I realize now I should have told you sooner. But… please, just sit. I will give you the answers you seek." He gestured at the plush chair in front of his desk.

I compile begrudgingly. The fact that he hadn't denied anything was still sinking in. I gripped the edge of the chair, grateful for something to hold on to.

"Do you remember what I told you about how Apep became our enemy?" he asked.

Of course I did. I had been warned of his power many times over the years. "Why are you asking me this?"

"Please, daughter, humor me."

I shrugged. "For light to exist, there must be darkness for it to fill. Amun realized there was not balance in the universe, so he created Apep."

My father nodded. "He was never supposed to cause chaos. Apep was meant to reign over the dark as I reign over the light—to keep the stars in the sky and ensure that the moon rises after the sun sets."

"But that wasn't enough for him," I said in a monotone voice, as though reciting a children's story.

"It seemed to be at first. In the beginning, he remained dedicated to his position as I was to mine. But as mortals began to populate the Earth, and more gods came to be, he grew jealous of the attention others received. Although he had a temple, Amun asked him to remain in the underworld and manage the darkness even when the mortal plane had light. He didn't get the festivals, the interaction most of us have with the people." He gestured toward a painting on the wall, depicting the first Summer Solstice festival.

"Uh-huh," I muttered, staring at the ceiling painted with tiny suns. I could recite the story by heart.

"After the god Set's banishment from Heliopolis for killing his brother, he traveled to the underworld. Amun regrets it now, but he had assumed his stance from humanity and being constrained to the darkness might not cause more chaos. But he was the one who infected Apep with that chaos. He put ideas into his head."

"He told them together, 'They could take the power they deserve'." I tapped my foot impatiently. "And so you prepared to stop them."

"Yes, I tried to stop them…but as I reached the location of his current lair, Amun intervened. He foresaw that a battle between us would lead to mutually assured destruction—for us and for the Earth."

Suddenly, he fell silent. For a moment, he seemed far away, staring out the window as if he saw the memory playing out in front of him.

"If Apep perished, there would be no one to control the darkness. After that night, he proposed something to me—a plan for my protection. He would create children for me: someone to protect me, and another who could fill in for me. Until a time of peace could be achieved, my family and I would be responsible for rising with the sun."

I rubbed my temple, growing tired of listening to something I could have recited myself. "Yes, and then we got cursed. But you have been looking for this peace, *right*? A solution?" I pressed, grateful for an opportunity to get the conversation back on track.

He looked back at me, taking a deep breath before speaking. "Bastet, there is more to the story."

Clearly.

"You must understand…after what happened to your mother…I had to be sure. I am unwilling to put you or your sister in any danger. But I did search, tirelessly, every day. I convinced myself this was temporary. And then, a few years ago…"

My father did not mention my mother often. Normally, I would've assured him that we knew that he kept us safe, she would be proud, and offer some kind of platitude. But I didn't have one at that moment.

"Before Apep lost his way, he had a wife," he continued.

My ears perked up at this, although I wasn't ready to tell him about my meeting with Tawaret yet. *If he can have secrets, so can I.*

"What happened to her?" I asked carefully, keeping my tone neutral.

"That's what I'm getting to. Before Apep's banishment, he and his wife had a child—a daughter, around your age. They did not go with him but stayed behind. Amun agreed to let them live on the outskirts, away from the society of gods, under the condition that they never interacted with us or with mortals."

Maybe meeting me had put her at risk. Guilt pricked at me.

"I didn't want to get you and Sekhmet's hopes up, you see—"

He glanced toward the portrait of the three of us that hung near the door, as his sentence trailed off without an ending.

"I don't understand." I furrowed my brow, my muscles tensing. *Why would a child of Apep be good news?*

My father looked back at me again. "Even though Keket was around your age, I personally was not aware of her until a few years ago. Amun had sent a messenger to check on them, and they reported back with some interesting findings. The child showed great promise in the development of her powers. We hoped maybe she could even take over the role of god of darkness from her father."

My shoulders dropped with relief. "That's wonderful news!" I exclaimed. "That means we can move forward, no mutually assured destruction!" A strange mix of confusion and excitement coursed through me. *Why would he hide this from me? And is this why Tawaret wanted to meet with me? Does she want her daughter to rise to power?*

My father sighed. "That was what I hoped. Wanting guidance on the best way to move forward, I went to see Thoth."

This made sense; many a god went to him for guidance, hoping for answers from either the past or whispers of the future.

"And what did he say?" I asked eagerly.

"As it turns out, he had recently received a prophecy. I hoped to leave with information about that prophecy that would strengthen us, that I could bring home and tell you and Sekhmet that the end was on the horizon. But instead, what I learned chilled me."

I froze. What could scare my father, one of the most powerful gods in existence?

He took a moment before he spoke. "Bastet, there is only one who can fight and destroy Apep. It is you."

Suddenly, I felt lightheaded. *Is the room moving?* My breath caught in my throat. "What are you…" I couldn't find words to finish my sentence as they escaped from my grasp.

"Daughter, I didn't want to accept it at first either. But the prophecy was clear."

"You're sure?" My chest tightened.

My father had always promised that he would be the one to fight for our freedom. That our service we had done on behalf of him, and the Egyptian people—was our duty, not a fight with chaos itself. I had never considered this reality.

"I wish I wasn't."

And suddenly, I regretted asking anything at all. I wanted to go back to the Solstice, to shake myself by the shoulders, tell her not to meet Tawaret, just enjoy the time with friends.

It wasn't too late, though—I could just walk out the door and pretend this conversation had never happened.

I had demanded answers, and now I had them. No one else was coming to end this fight for me. What was I going to do, pretend nothing had changed?

And hadn't I always been a part of this? Every night, I took up my spear and defended my father and the people of Egypt. I was not a helpless little girl. *I can't just give up.*

"I can do this," I told him, straightening up in my seat, willing my words to sound strong. "You can train me, Sekhmet can train—"

"Daughter, surely you understand that it is not that simple?" His frown deepened.

"There is only one who can destroy Apep, and it's me, it all seems quite simple actually," I replied. The fear was starting to dissipate, filled with the realization that I could actually be free if I did this. If risking my life is what it takes to win our freedom, then so be it—I am ready to give everything.

"Yes, but the prophecy made no promise of victory, Bastet. It is not a foretelling of the future, this message Thoth received. If anything, it felt more like a warning."

Isn't a prophecy more of a promise? It is a foretelling of the future, not a guess. Why must he assume the worst? "A warning of what?"

"A warning that any attempts I make alone, any attempt of the gods of Egypt made will fail. That, for reasons even the god of wisdom himself can't explain, only if you strike the final blow can Apep be defeated."

"Then don't go without me," I insisted. My hands clenched together. This was so obvious. *Does he view me as useless?*

"I will not put you in that kind of danger," my father insisted, finality in his tone; the matter had already been decided. "You are not ready. Maybe one day…"

I grunted, shaking my head. "Everything with you is always *someday*, be patient, how can I possibly still trust you?"

"Wait…" I said, a thought suddenly nagging me as I remembered all the times he had brushed me off. "How long have you known?"

"Of the prophecy?" He hesitated. His voice sounded apologetic. "Thoth received the revelation around three years ago."

I felt like a slap in the face.

"So…" I repeated, my voice began to rise. "You have known for three years that there was, in fact, a way to defeat Apep—and you kept it from me. Not just me! You hid this from Sekhmet. You let me believe you were out searching for answers, when you weren't looking at all." *Why had I been so naive? So trusting?*

"Bastet, I did not hide this for selfish reasons," he insisted, his voice hardening. "I am your father, and when the time was right, I would've told you. I still hope there might be another solution, I just…haven't found it yet."

"Has there ever been a time, in all of history, where something that didn't align with Thoth's prophecy came to pass?" I held out my arms and pointed toward the various paintings on the wall that depicted famous scenes of our history.

"No," he admitted. "But just because something has been true does not mean it always will. That is the nature of the present—and the hope of the future."

"You don't even believe that," I scoffed.

"You do not get to speak to me that way," he snapped, his volume rising to match mine. "I was protecting you and your sister; that is what I will always do."

"Really? I thought I was protecting you. Or isn't that why Sekhmet and I were created? Just to get you out of a bind?"

"Daughter, enough. My patience is running out."

I stood up. "I can't believe I had to find out the truth from our enemy and not my own father," I scoffed.

"What are you talking about?"

"Tawaret, she came to find me. *She* decided I deserve to hear the truth." I eased the door open and paused, listening, before stepping outside.

"You spoke with her? How…When…? Bastet, this conversation is not over. Sit back down!"

"No, but thanks for coming clean with me, I suppose. I can handle the rest all on my own."

I stepped out into the hallway and slammed the door behind me.

7

THE WAR ROOM

As I ran from my father's office, my eyes watered. I leaned against a pillar, drew a deep breath, and tried to keep them dry. The reality of what I'd done hit me. I couldn't fathom that I had spoken to the ancient sun of the god that way—father or not.

I slammed the door! Anyone else would've met with a fury I didn't want to picture.

Before composing myself, I saw Ptah walking toward me.

Wanting a moment alone, I slipped behind the column to try and hide myself, but it was too late.

"Bast, what is wrong?" Ptah's eyes widened with concern as he stepped in front of me.

"Oh, Ptah…" The moisture spilled into tears. My instinct was to fight them off. I shouldn't be crying in front of anyone, not even a close friend. It was a sign of weakness that the gods tried to leave for mortals.

But this was not the first time he had seen me cry.

* * *

The first time Ptah saw me cry happened near the start of our friendship.

We had plans to meet up later that night, but first I had dinner with my family.

Something seemed off from the start. My father acted only half present—he kept staring at the wall, slow to respond to anyone, even the servants.

Once the main dish was cleared, he set down his silverware and coughed, grabbing our attention.

"Daughters, you may soon hear some…news. But I want you to hear it from me first."

I exchanged a look with Sekhmet, biting my lip. She had her arms crossed, face blank.

"We have brought your mother's killer to justice," he informed us.

I felt my muscles tense. "I…I thought you haven't been able to figure out who killed her."

Ra shook his head. "I wanted to keep you safe. I was worried you might take matters into your own hands if I told you."

In retrospect, he had been hiding things from us for a long time.

"That's ridiculous," Sekhmet retorted. "We have never not followed your orders." It was one of the only times I'd ever heard her speak to him like that.

I expected him to rebuke her, but he did not. "I couldn't risk it. I already lost your mother to…" he sighed. "It is time I told you the full story."

He lied to us?

"Your mother, she never felt right about agreeing to Amen's…terms. It was easy to say yes before we met you. But after you were born, we both felt an immense amount of guilt—guilt for signing you up for a life of service to my court alone, for the limits placed on your lives."

He had never said that before.

"I promised I would figure something out," he continued. "But she did not want you forming memories of the life we had set you up for. She wanted you to grow up normally."

I wished—not for the first time or the last-that I could speak with her, even for a moment. To tell her that I could manage.

"But she decided to take matters into her own hands. She tried to speak with Apep directly. To make a deal, to offer him power or some of her magic—anything to end this feud so that Amun could release you from the arrangement."

"Foolish…" Sekhmet whispered. I hear her sniff.

"Set struck her down before she even reached Apep," our father explained. "He used a sword enchanted with ancient, forbidden magic…" His words caught in his throat.

"I am ashamed it took me this long to bring him to justice," he continued. "But my soldiers found him and brought him to Anubis for judgment. He has been wiped from his world."

"Our mother died because of us?" I asked, tears already welling up in my eyes. Our father was an ancient god of great power; he had many enemies. We had always assumed that was why he could not figure out the identity of the killer.

"Do not blame yourself," Ra insisted. "She made her decision out of love, and if I could ask her now…I am certain she would do the same thing again. And now Set is dead, with no chance at peace."

In a rare break of composure, Sekhmet stood up from the table and fled the room.

My father and I remained at the table while I tried to keep my tears quiet. "Is Mother at peace, at least?" I asked. It was something I had wondered for a long time, too afraid to ask.

He nodded. "Yes. Anubis has confirmed it." The god of death did not often reveal his rulings, but I was not surprised he broke that rule for my father.

"I should go after her," I said, after a moment of silence.

I had every intention of doing so. But I found my feet carried me away from the palace and toward Ptah's instead.

I found him sitting outside—he loved to watch architecture and nature for ideas.

He didn't question why I showed up there unannounced. He saw me crying and pulled me in a hug. We stood there in the moonlight for a long time. Once my tears were dry, I told him everything.

"Somehow finding out she died for us feels the same as when I first found out she passed," I told him. "It's a fresh cut."

"You have no reason to feel guilty," he insisted. The same words my father used, but it was easier to trust the words coming from him.

"I just wish I had the chance to talk to her one more time, does that make sense? Even for a moment. It's not fair; the whole point of immortality is that we aren't supposed to deal with death. Gods don't grow up without parents."

I regretted it as soon as I said it. Ptah hadn't grown up without parents—he'd never had them.

But he showed no resentment. "No, they normally don't."

I stayed with him at that bench until dawn, when inevitably, my eyes closed.

I woke up that night in my own bed—Ptah had carried me home.

I leaned against the column as the memory faded. That day was strikingly similar to this one, wasn't it?

My father had told me lies, I cried, and Ptah was here.

If the past was any indicator, telling him was a good idea. For some reason, he always made my mental load lighter and helped me smile. But I didn't want to feel better, not yet. I was too angry, and I wanted that—the anger, the sadness—to propel me into action I might not otherwise take.

Ptah was still watching me, his tone soft. "Did your father say something?"

I turned away. "I'm sorry, but I'm not ready to talk about it yet." I wiped my eyes.

I tried not to notice the hurt visible in his eyes at being brushed off. "Alright, but you know you can, right?"

"Yes," I acknowledged. "But there's someone I need to speak with first."

8

TRUANCY

The next night when I woke up, I went through the motions of getting ready for my usual duties. But as I stood in front of the mirror, holding my armored vest made of thick leather, I couldn't bring myself to put it on. Why should I? After everything I learned yesterday, what's the point?

Instead, I tossed it aside and stared at the plain tunic I wore underneath it in the reflection. What would a normal morning be like for the average young goddess?

"For one thing, I'd probably have more interesting clothes to choose from," I muttered, eyeing the bare selection that hung out of my small closet. Outside of rare festivals or solstices, I only wore what was practical. Jewelry was out of the question—too much risk of it interfering with my duties.

Henet once told me that, at school, her classmates often discussed each other's outfits— the gods of beauty and apparel would determine what was popular amongst the masses. I couldn't imagine holding a single conversation about that, because I'd never worn anything that wasn't chosen for me by someone else.

Tired of staring at myself, I walked across the hallway to Sekhmet's room. We woke up at the same time, so she would still be there.

I knocked softly on the door. "Sister?"

"Come in," she called.

Sekhmet's room was much neater than mine, everything organized and put in a place that felt intentional. You could see her half of the rugs the goddess Neith had gifted to us, its intricate design depicting the creation story. She put down the stack of documents she'd been sorting and looked at me. "Yes, Bastet?"

"I'm going to ask you something, and I can guess what you're going to say, but I request you to have an open mind…"

"Strong start," Sekhmet remarked.

"I want a day off," I blurted.

Sekhmet snorted. "Have you lost your mind?"

I figured she would say that.

I crossed my arms. "No, I just…I need a minute to breathe, away from everything." If I was being honest, I would have said I didn't want to see our father.

"What if something happens?" she asked. "This is not my duty, you are uniquely equipped with your shield power, and…we are talking about the safety of the sun here."

"You're a better fighter though." There was no way she'd argue with that. "If Apep attacks, which never happens, you would protect the ship and the sun better than I could."

She tapped her foot, clearly considering my words. But then she stopped and shook her head. "I won't put our father at risk like that."

"Like he does to us?" I snapped.

She pursed her lips. "Something's happened, hasn't it? Something you're not telling me."

I smoothed a wrinkle from my tunic, debating what to say.

She took a step closer to me, her voice soft. "Sister, please."

She deserves to know.

But I hadn't said it out loud yet. Doing so would make it more real—the betrayal that had pierced my heart, the pressure that now weighed down my shoulders with my newfound responsibility.

I gulped. "Father has been hiding something from us. I…perhaps you should sit down."

She narrowed her eyes but obliged.

I told her everything—from meeting Tawaret, speaking with the advisors, and finally confronting our father. The only thing I left out was crying in Ptah's arms.

It was good Sekhmet had sat down. I could tell she was in shock, blinking rapidly and eyes clouded. "This doesn't make any sense," she insisted, staring at the wall.

"How long has he known?" The pitch of her voice sounded higher than normal.

"A couple of years, I believe? Since he discovered the existence of Keket."

Her hand gripped the edge of the desk. "Alright, I will take your place."

"Really?" It was not the reaction I had expected. I assumed she would defend him, assure me there was some reason we didn't understand, that our duty to Egypt eclipsed everything else.

But instead, she stood up. "I want to speak with him myself. You…do what it is you wish."

What did I wish to do? What a strange thing to consider. I stood back in my room, lingering in front of my closet again.

I could message Ptah, but he'd only worry. He already had been worried about me the day before. I wanted to hang out with someone who I knew wouldn't ask any questions. Plus…the way he had looked at me was something I wasn't ready to reflect on.

So I sent an ibis bird to Henet instead, asking her to meet me. Luckily, she was much easier to convince than Sekhmet, and within a few minutes, she sent a return message, agreeing to meet me.

Grinning, I grabbed one of my festival dresses. I'd probably be overdressed for wherever we went, but I didn't care.

I ran down the stairs, excitement buzzing through me.

Henet waited outside the living quarters, humming to herself. She was dressed more casually, but I knew she'd be too polite to comment on my choice of attire.

Seeing me, she held out her hands, gesturing into the night. "Alright, so you have a whole day off," she declared. "What are we doing?"

"I want to do something normal," I declared, as though the word itself had magic power. "What do you normally do on a day off? No school, no journeys with me, just fun?"

She clasped her hands together, taking a moment, then holding her index finger out excitedly.

"Have you ever ridden a celestial horse?" She asked me.

I shook my head. "No, but that sounds fantastic. Tell me more."

We headed into town toward the vendors who served the gods (mostly half-gods). The path was well lit, allowing me to take in all the vibrant colors of the stalls. I loved that each of them looked a little different, some large tents, others just a table with a little hand-painted sign.

Immortals rarely needed to shop for anything. Temples provided food, cloth, and daily necessities. Our bodies hardly changed, so clothes accumulated rather than wore out. Food was more for energy and ka levels than survival.

This meant shopping for an immortal person was an activity done not out of necessity, but of fun.

The stalls mainly hosted artisans. There were no farming tools or baking ingredients here. My eyes widened at the huge paintings and elaborate rugs.

"Isn't the music wonderful?" Henet asked. "Most of them are quite talented, hoping to be hired as in-house court artisan. My father once employed someone from here."

"There's so many people!" I remarked, nearly overwhelmed by the chatter and music.

She laughed. "Yes, it's part of the fun. Here, I have to show you something!" She led me down to a section marked with a sign reading "Entertainment."

"Whoa…" I breathed. A stadium full of people watched half-gods hurl javelins at painted targets. Each successful throw was greeted by roaring cheers and a booming announcer calling out scores.

By the time we got to the stables—I had nearly forgotten why we'd come, distracted by the beautiful singers, the stalls, the excitement. But the horses' whinnies brought me back.

Henet dragged me to the woman at the front. "We will take one celestial horse trek each," she said, throwing down some gold coins when rattled hitting the surface of the counter.

The woman took the money. "Of course, follow me."

I had seen mortal horses from afar, but celestial rattled, dwarfed them in size, standing an impressive foot or so taller than any regular horse I'd seen. They were also wider, but what set them apart the most were the wings. They appeared to be semi-translucent, meaning it took me a moment to notice them, but once I did, it was the only thing I could see.

"They're beautiful," I whispered.

Henet giggled. "Isn't it wonderful? That's what makes them so special!"

I let the attendant boost me into the saddle, and I landed awkwardly, clutching the mane until I steadied myself.

"Please hold on to the reins at all times and remain secure in your saddle," she instructed.

I had never been so high up. Everything looked so tiny! The market was shrinking beneath last conversations, the lights blurring together.

"How do you feel?" Henet shouted over the rushing wind.

I was starting to feel a little faint, so I looked forward instead of down. "Everything is so small…"

She spread her arms for a moment—terrifying me—before reclaiming the reins. "I know? It's wonderful. When I'm up here, I imagine my problems are so small, maybe they'll just float away by the time I land."

I knew my problems remained too heavy to just float away, but something about the vast openness of the world was electrifying. I had never been outside of Heliopolis. I had barely considered the lands beyond.

But from the sky, they felt so close, like if I really wanted to, I could fly this horse to the other side of the world.

"What is it like?" I asked, after a few more minutes. "To be able to go anywhere you want. To have infinite time?"

Henet arched an eyebrow. "Do you presume that's what the rest of us have, Bastet?"

I flushed. "I mean not infinite, but you know what I mean…"

"My friend, I am grateful for my life, but no one is free to do whatever they want or go wherever they want. We all have duties, most of us just don't have duties as important as yours."

The next night, I boarded the Meneset as usual. I polished my spear as my father got on board, nervously keeping my eyes down and avoiding his gaze. I was not excited for whatever lecture I would likely receive for the previous night's actions.

But he said nothing. He got into his normal position as if I weren't even there.

The silent treatment?

As if Duat itself agreed to the silence, no mortals sought guidance that night. The entire journey stayed everyone stayed quiet, and while that silence felt heavier than normal, it gave me time to think. Even Henet and I barely spoke— only sharing a brief smile.

The night before, I had stayed up until Sekhmet returned. She wouldn't reveal the details of her conversation with our father. But she did tell me that while she understood my request, she stood by her original conditions. She was willing to help, but we needed a plan—something concrete before we entered a fight.

In order to come up with a plan, I needed to hear the prophecy for myself. I had anticipated a fight with my father first, but if I could skip that part, all the better for me.

The moment we docked, I prepared to head straight for Thoth's temple. Tonight was his weekly audience, meaning no courtiers to delay me. He held knowledge of the future and the past, and I needed to learn from both.

As the boat hit the sand, I jumped out as planned. But before I could leave, Father spoke to me.

"Bastet, a moment."

I stopped, but I did not turn around.

"Is this life truly not enough for you? At least for now?" His voice was pained.

I whipped my head around. "You weren't listening at all if your conclusion is that this is all about my own life. The sun itself is at risk, all of Egypt! You constantly speak of your own duty to our people, and you really don't understand that?"

He sighed. "I can't stop you from pursuing this, can I?"

"No." Truthfully, he could have, of course— with his power and connections—but the fact that he asked mattered. It just wasn't enough.

"When Sekhmet showed up instead of you yesterday, initially I was angry. I did not raise a daughter of mine to shirk her responsibilities. But I see now that I…created this problem, by hiding this all from you. Can I at least ask you to be careful? Promise me you won't charge blindly through the underworld looking for a fight."

"All I am doing at this moment is finding the prophecy you kept hidden from me." I did not add that I wanted to act as soon as I could convince Sekhmet to join me.

"It is unlikely that is truly what you mean… and this isn't our last conversation. Do you understand?

I nodded.

"But I will no longer stand in your way."

9

PROPHECY

You do not just stroll in and make demands of an ancient god. One must choose their words carefully.

Therefore I walked to Thoth's temple slowly, carefully forming a sentence that sounded both confident and respectful.

It was important I did not show disrespect to my father in this inquiry, despite how I might feel. "My father has graciously shared with me the existence of the prophecy involving the slaying of Apep—More specifically, that I am the only one who can defeat him."

Thoth's temple was second in size only to Ra's. Just as my family's temple represented our patronage to the sun, his represented that of the moon. Instead of our tall windows, a glass ceiling let the viewer see the stars unobstructed. The torches lining the silver limestone walls were lit with blue-tinted flame.

I'd always been a bit jealous of the clothes his court wore, garments that reflected the spirit of the moon. The priests who passed me wore robes of deep blue with silver accents.

While everything here contrasted with Ra's court, the two had never been enemies. The gods understood the importance of both the moon and the sun for the good of our world.

I walked straight to Thoth's audience room, one of the first visible upon entering the grand entrance hall. It was easy to recognize: a line of other gods and half-gods stood there seeking his guidance.

A priest stood at the door, opening it only when it was someone's turn, then closing it behind them. Thoth had always put a great emphasis on privacy. Prophecies were to be heard only by those involved, and no one else. Lest, the future itself be put at risk.

When my turn arrived, I nodded at the priest and entered. The room was even bigger than I had expected. It was long, with thousands of scrolls and books lining the walls. The sight made my father's collection look tiny. Above the shelves lay hieroglyphics—the earliest letters barely recognizable to me. This was the history of writing itself, right before my eyes.

I approached Thoth on top of a silver rug whose width matched the window above, the moonlight seeming to light my steps. It was not a short walk, but I used the time to repeat my words once again.

Thoth sat on a giant silver throne, its carvings matching the celestial glyphs overhead. Statues representing the different phases of the moon stood on either side of him.

Has it always been that big? I suddenly felt a foot shorter, craning my neck just to see his face.

Thoth was in his human form, though his head was that of an ibis—the very birds he had created. While the birds came in a variety of colors, his were a grayish blue, and His bill was a dark green curve.

He radiated confidence and authority, his arms resting wide and comfortably across the throne's armrests. He sat perfectly still until I stopped walking.

"Daughter of Ra," he greeted me. His deep voice echoed throughout the hall.

I bowed my head slightly. "Thoth, thank you for providing me with an audience."

"What discernment can I provide to you?"

Suddenly, everything I had practiced fled my mind. "I was recently informed there is a prophecy regarding the god of chaos, the sun, and well…myself."

That could have gone better.

He nodded. "I foresaw this day was soon arriving." He gestured for me to continue.

Now's the moment—you can recover.

I couldn't exactly match the volume of his voice, but met his eyes and spoke clearly, finally releasing the words I had practiced. "I am here today to request of you the prophecy in its full form, and additionally, any historical texts regarding those who have previously fought Apep and did not succeed."

"And your father informed you of the risks of this venture?" he asked.

Why does everyone assume I am so clueless?

I worked to keep the frustration off my face. "I am aware of the risks. But I wish to free my sister and myself from our curse."

Thoth was unlikely to refuse me access to the prophecy as one of its subjects, but he was under no obligation to give me the additional historical texts. He knew my father had hidden this from me. What if my father instructed him to only show me partial truths?

He paused and tilted his head as if weighing me. In a moment of silence, his gaze swept over me. Was he trying to decide whether I could handle it?

Finally, he responded. "Very well."

I took a deep breath, relief washed over me. "Thank you."

Thoth nodded. "Upon your exit, wait at the podium in the hallway. The scrolls you need will appear there shortly, and you may borrow them. They must be returned within a fortnight to maintain the sanctity of the text. Remember this." He gestured toward a side door on the right.

Thoth did not believe in copies. Copies could be lost, corrupted—or worse, spread where they did not belong.

"Yes, I will make every effort to return them as soon as possible." I started walking toward the door, eager to collect the scrolls.

"And Bastet," he added, his tone softer. "I wish you the luck of many gods, for you will need it."

The sheer number of scrolls that accompanied me home surprised me. In a way, they gave some credibility to my father's words. They proved that he had indeed tried to take down the chaos. Some of the records were a bit grim—priests and half-gods taken down by poisonous bites from the snake god. A few were even swallowed whole.

At least, with so many accounts, I could rule out certain tactics. One group had attempted to stun Apep with a spell, but it failed—the shape of his serpentine spine rendered it useless. When they dropped their defenses to cast it, he simply swished his tail and pushed them into the ocean.

Another account told of a chameleon half-god who waited an hour in the dark before striking. He severed Apep's tail with a sword, expecting the pain to give the others an opening to strike. But Apep's tail grew back.

Needing a break from the bleak reports, I turned to the prophecy.

The parchment was papyrus but unlike any in everyday use—colored a silver reminiscent of Thoth's temple, with blue coating lining the edges. As I unrolled it, it floated above me of its own accord.

I stepped back as Thoth's voice started booming from the scroll, which now glowed brightly. My heart pounded, my eyes transfixed as the words lit up one by one as he spoke them aloud:

It is prophesied that the chaos god will slither
In between the world of life and death
Unless a conqueror comes forth

And the daughters of Ra remain
Cursed to live only in the dark.
There is only one who may rise to this task
The daughter who rides with the sun.

If she fights true, with the magic within
She may finally step into the light.
Should she fail, the sky will turn red
With the blood of an unprotected sun—
And chaos will take hold.

If she succeeds, *then a new champion*
Must rise to guard the night—
The daughter of the darkness.

These events must take place before
The latter's coming of age
Or the curse that binds one to the day
And keeps another from the night
Will last without end.

My father had not exaggerated the prophecy's intensity.

As the voice faded, the parchment dropped to the floor. I did not catch it. I stood frozen in place as the words reverberated in my head. There was no turning back now.

For a fleeting moment, I was no longer angry with him. After all, how would I react if the prophecy mentioned him or Sekhmet? But it passed quickly. I still deserved to know. It's not as if Thoth would issue a new prophecy to cancel this one out. These were the facts, and it was time someone in the family faced them.

Two days later, I was still spending every free moment in the library. The piles of books I had read (or occasionally skimmed) accumulated next to me, growing larger with each passing hour.

What would my sister consider a plan?

Today, I had decided to study wars of the past.

The battles of humans seemed included mostly as excuses for gods to show off the times they used their powers to intervene in the conflicts of man. For example, there were those that aided in the famous battle of Ramses II versus the Hittites—a war that ended in the world's first peace treaty. Ramses II was losing before he channeled Set, who helped him save his people.

Every time I saw a name, I stopped and put my finger on it, committing it to memory. I wasn't surprised to see Sekhmet's friend Montu. I'll have to ask her to talk to him. Sobek's name appeared quite a few times; the crocodile god applauded for both strength and strategy.

But unless I spoke to them, these were just names, they offered no clear way to defeat Apep where Ra's priests and fighters had failed.

I was about to leave when I spotted a small book at the end of the shelf. It was written by a child of Renenutet, goddess of agriculture. Her son, Thermouth, had been governor of a small city in the Nile, struck by drought. Desperate to save his people, Thermouth called upon his mother, who in turn petitioned Heka, the god of magic. Heka granted Thermouth temporary power—neither knowing what it would be. Fortunately, it allowed him to bless the livestock with long, healthy lives. Their meat fed his people until the spring rains returned.

My eyes lit up as the story ignited a possibility that struck me—perhaps my powers did not have to wait until my ascension. I closed the book, feeling a sense of relief that my time here hadn't been wasted.

Perhaps Heka could simply unlock them. Like Thermouth, I did not know what they would take, but surely as the daughter of Ra they would be powerful—useful, even.

It wasn't exactly the kind of plan Sekhmet might approve of, but as I left with a book on summoning Heka, I felt lighter. At least now, I had an idea.

10

HEKA

No one knew the location of Heka's temple. People said his abundance of spells and secrets made him paranoid. And so, he transported herself there by teleportation. His court and priests traveled in much the same way, summoned to mysterious locations where they would speak an incantation and shift to the temple.

As such, the only way to contact him was to offer a magical sacrifice. Some records claim he absorbed them, strengthening his power and learning new spells from them. Others declared he simply hoards them away, reveling in the power he held over his fellow gods.

It had to be something meaningful. A simple gift of meat or wine—a mortal's offering—would not be enough to pique his interest. In fact, Heka never interacted with mortals at all. He did not believe they deserved magic.

I placed the amulet my father had given me on an altar in the sand. Next to it, I spelled Heka's name in stones. a twinge of guilt pulled at me, but I ignored it. I had little else to offer. My father would certainly not approve, but hopefully he would one day understand.

With the altar set up, I bowed my head and held out my hands toward the altar and spoke the words of summoning. "Heka, god of magic, I, goddess Bastet, call to you. I request your grand intercession and have provided this sacrifice, which I hope you find acceptable, to grant me an audience.

Minutes passed in silence. I became painfully aware of the chill in the night air and began to wonder if I had done something wrong. *What even happens if you perform an incantation wrong? What if someone—or something—else shows up?* My muscles tensed. I was completely alone. Could I even defend myself?

I shook the thoughts away. Did the text say anything about how long it was supposed to take?

I almost considered going back inside to review the summoning text, but then the altar began to glow. A moment later, Heka appeared in front of me.

He was a huge god, with a fully human body and head.

Isn't that a bit ironic.

On his head sat a crown topped with two golden snakes coiled around a small staff, slithering endlessly around each other. They moved so quickly that it was almost difficult to look at, and the sight made me uncomfortable.

I had read the headpiece served as a trophy from a serpent he had slayed long before I was born. It was part of why I realized he had to be the one to help me on my quest.

"Bastet, you have called upon me." His voice was powerful, filling the air as if we stood in a great hall rather than beneath the open sky.

"Thank you for answering my call," I responded, bowing my head again in respect.

"I am fascinated to hear from a child of Ra," he replied, crossing his arms and leaning against the altar.

"Yes, well, I believe you to be the only deity who can aid my plight." I'd heard he responded well to flattery.

My instincts turned out to be right, as he smiled at that. "You're probably right about that. What do you seek from the god of magic?"

I walked closer, although only by a foot. Truth be told, I was scared to get too close. "I request your aid in discovering my divine power." I gestured toward the offering I had brought on the altar.

He raised an eyebrow. "You are not yet fully a god."

I was just glad he didn't laugh at me.

"Yes, but under extraordinary circumstances, half-gods have been granted access to their full powers. As a creation of Amun, I believe my unique situation qualifies me for the same." At least, I sure hope so.

"Interesting." he said thoughtfully. "Something I hadn't considered."

I made sure to work in another compliment. "Your rules over magic have worked expertly for centuries, which is why I am certain you will see the reason in my request."

Heka rubbed his chin. "You are correct—my methods have worked out quite well. Well then, if you wish to be considered a half-god, I will ask you the same question I ask of them. What extraordinary circumstance do you believe makes you worthy of bearing divine magic?"

Is this going well? "After receiving a prophecy from the god of wisdom, I have discovered that I am destined to be the conqueror of Apep. I do not believe this to be possible without the gift of your magic unlocked within me." I put my hand on my heart.

"I suppose that does count as extra ordinary." He clapped his hands together. "Very well Bastet, I will help you unlock your power. But if you should fail in this venture—your powers will once again be locked within you."

I refrained from telling him that if I failed, Egypt would have far greater concerns than me losing powers.

Heka snapped his fingers. The altar glowed, and then cleared. My amulet disappeared, fading away. Based on what I'd read, it was teleported back to his temple. I instinctively put my hand to my neck, which was now empty. How am I going to explain this?

In place of my offerings appeared four golden flasks. Each contained a swirling, colored liquid embossed with a symbol: orange with a lightning bolt, green with an eye, blue with an ocean wave, and red with a flame.

He gestured toward them. "Most half-gods have an inkling of their power at birth. But since you have only what Amun gifted to you—we must first discover your inner power. These gifts represent the possibilities I believe suit you best based on the facts of your creation."

I found myself in front of the altar, almost in a trance, unsure if I moved of my own will or was drawn by an invisible force attached to the goblets.

"Drink the one that calls to your soul, and we will find your answer." He instructed in a deep voice, watching me intently. I noticed a glow around his pupils. The snakes began to move more slowly, as if they too were watching intently.

I closed my eyes, breathed deeply, and shut everything out but the goblets below. When I opened them, the green liquid called to me. Its scent was the sweetest smell I had ever encountered. I picked it up and held it to my lips, pausing for a moment.

What if this is poisoned? Sekhmet would call me foolish, for drinking something from a god I had never met before.

But I yearned to taste it, the sensation rather overwhelming.

Luckily, it tasted as sweet as it smelled— warm, like tea, mixed with a bit of lemon. The soothing warmth spread down my throat.

Suddenly the ground below me trembled. Images flashed in my mind, blurry, as if trying to recall a childhood memory. It felt as if I was dreaming, but I was certainly awake, I could feel a strong breeze on my face. I saw Sekhmet, sitting in her war room. My vision stayed on her only for a moment. Then I saw my father, in his meeting room with his advisors. My right eye tingled slightly. "What is this?" I asked.

Heka was smiling. "You, Bastet, have been gifted with the all-seeing eye."

"What?" I asked as I blinked, trying to shake off the images. They did not disappear so much as recede beneath the surface.

"Your right eye no longer sees only what lies before you. It now sees what you seek, and what you are connected to."

I touched my head, which was aching. I wasn't sure if it was from the visions or Heka's strange words.

I forced myself to concentrate on what he was saying. Connected to… "Is that why I see my family?"

"Yes, Blood ties make them easier to find. But you will be able to locate others as well."

Easy? This does not feel easy.

"Alright, well how do I control this?" I thought of someone with whom I had no ties and tried to locate Thoth, but only saw a haze.

"It will take practice," he explained. "It helps when you have an emotional connection with the person. The connections of the heart are just as strong as those of blood—though we don't always realize that."

"Connections of our heart…" I repeated, still processing his words.

A part of me was disappointed, though I tried not to show it. How was this power supposed to help me slay the great god of chaos? It wasn't exactly a bolt of lightning or the fire represented on some of the other goblets.

Heka clearly saw through me. "Bastet, I can only help beings unlock their power—I do not choose it. That is left to Amun, and he would not grant you a gift with no purpose."

"Yes, but—"

"Besides," he interrupted, "is it not true that Apep has grown harder to find? That no one knows where his lair presently resides?"

"Yes, that is true," I intoned. Sure, that was one small piece of the puzzle I hadn't worked out yet. But finding him was not enough.

The snakes on Heka's head sped up as he titled his head. "Does the prophecy say you must defeat him alone?"

I thought back to the words now etched in my memory. "No, I suppose it does not. It simply says I must be the one to offer the killing blow."

"Trust in Amun's gift, it will serve you well— along with the knowledge of those who came before you."

"Came before me? what does that mean?" I had never heard or read of anyone with a locating power—though a small part of me still hoped there was more to the eye than that.

"The All-Seeing Eye you have been gifted with, is one of many forms of the Eye of Ra," he explained. "Others have shared this gift, and others will. Hathor is one such example."

I groaned. "Of course she is."

Heka raised an eyebrow but did not inquire further. "Bastet, it is time for me to take my leave. I wish you good luck."

I was beginning to tire of that phrase.

That day, I dreamt of following someone through a dense forest. A force pulled me forward, guiding me down a path I instinctively recalled, though I did not know who I was following. Each time I neared my goal—marked by a clearing or a trail of footprints—fog would roll in, and I would find myself back at the forest's edge.

95

11

A MENTOR

It was not difficult to find Hathor. As a favored guest of Ra, she had moved her daily operations to a wing of his temple, although she still had her own, as she was not married to my father—yet.

Some referred to Hathor as a "queen god". This was not the compliment it may appear on the surface. No, instead, it referenced her powers of music, dance, and beauty. She had founded and continued to manage the majority of the festivals in Heliopolis.

As I expected, Hathor was in her office, who ushered me in right away when I knocked.

The room was chock full of decor-paintings lining the wall from top to bottom, with space only existing to make room for a sculpture or fancy vase. Her desk was huge; you would have to stand to properly access the whole surface covered in invites for events and planning documents.

"Bastet, I don't know if you've ever come to visit me before!" Hathor smiled, gesturing for me to sit across from her.

I took a seat in a plush silk chair and crossed my legs. She wasn't wrong. Hathor had invited Sekhmet and me many times to come and learn about her work, should we want to be involved when we came into our full powers. Neither of us did, of course, and it was easy to make excuses when you had access to only half the amount of time as everyone else.

"Well, I hope you don't mind I come to ask you a favor," I said, feeling a bit ashamed that I came only because of my own needs.

"I will certainly help if I can!"

I looked around, noticing a painting of all the ancient gods together, including Heka.

Surely this meant she respected him and was aware of what he could do. "I recently had the opportunity to meet with Heka and unlock some of my full powers…early."

It sounded ridiculously fake to me, but Hathor either didn't pick up on the awkwardness of my tone or simply didn't care. "How exciting! What is it?"

"I have become one of the several forms of the Eyes of Ra," I explained. "My specific powers, I do not have a grasp on the full extent of them yet, but they can help with locating. Heka mentioned you also are an extension of the Eye of Ra?"

She clapped her hands together, excited. "Yes! Before I grew…close to your father, I worked with him in defense, not too unlike yourself!"

That was news to me; I'd always wondered how they'd met. It was strange to picture her in a role like mine, instead of sitting at some desk, planning a party.

"Although not in Duat, of course. For a while, my title was actually 'Hathor of the Four Faces'. I was given the ability to see in four directions at once to help guard our borders before other gods came in to fulfill that role better than I. I could also see quite a distance away!" She seemed to remember this time fondly, smiling as she talked about it.

Four directions at once? The idea made my head hurt just imagining. "But you no longer have these abilities?"

Hathor put her hand on her chin, considering. "I believe I could unlock them again; there has simply been no need. Can I assume you would like some help using your new powers?"

She seemed quite nice—why did she have to be so nice? I couldn't stop myself from feeling relieved that not only did she want to help me, but she also wasn't asking intrusive questions about how I'd convinced Heka in the first place.

It was growing difficult to dislike her, something I could not admit to Sekhmet.

"Any training or guidance you provide would be most appreciated," I confirmed.

"Of course, I will ask Heka myself how to unlock my own eyesight abilities if I can't figure it out myself. This will be great; we can finally spend some time together!"

I was not surprised she turned this situation into an opportunity to "bond". But if I wanted to come back to Sekhmet and have her take me seriously, I would need more than just the announcement of a vague power I had no experience using. I had no choice, even though she would not like the source.

Smiling as wide as I could manage, I said, "Sounds great. Before we get started, would you be alright with keeping this a secret from my father for now? I want to surprise him with my new abilities!"

This was not exactly a lie. I hoped it would be a welcome surprise eventually, but if he found out about our training now, he would see it for exactly what it was—preparing for a fight he had no interest in me entering.

"Sure, sounds fun!" She believed me so earnestly, the guilty feeling began to return for misleading her.

And with that, I joined the Eyes of Ra.

Hathor greeted me a few nights later in one of the training rooms for new priests and magic wielders. It was meant to be a safe space for practice, with flat concrete flooring and soft walls in case someone was to be thrown at them.

I spent a lot of time there with Sekhmet as a child during our initial training, but I hadn't seen it in years. I had fond memories of those times, but it felt different now.

I wasn't here to use my basic shield or practice with the spear. I was here to learn an all-new power.

"So, what have you located so far with your eye?" Hathor asked.

"Well, not much really," I admitted. "When Heka first imbued me with the power, I was able to find those in my family without effort. But I haven't tried it on anyone else."

Hathor had some books in front of her. I recognized them as magic tomes. She ran her finger across some text and then asked, "And has your ka level shifted at all?"

"A little bit." I had noticed that. I usually went through most of my daily allotment of magical energy quickly, using my cat reflexes or wielding defense. But, when I was experimenting with my eye in Duat (as discreetly as possible), I noticed less overall energy being used.

"Hmmm…" She flipped through the pages. "How about objects? Have you tested that out yet?"

"You think I can find objects?" I wrinkled my forehead.

Hathor leaned forward. "Well, did Heka mention you couldn't?"

I shook my head. "No, but…" Honestly, this conversation made me wish I had asked him more questions. But Heka had been intimidating, and it had taken a while for my brain to even process what had happened.

Hathor snapped her book closed and grinned. "Alright, first lesson in magic. No god's powers are the same. The first thing I did when I got my powers? Try all sorts of things. How far I could see, if it was different depending on the time of day, if one eye was stronger than the other."

She looked off into the distance a bit, as if reviewing a memory. "It was actually quite fun."

"But what use would finding objects give me?" I questioned, regretting my tone a bit once the words left my mouth.

But Hathor did not seem offended. "Let's workshop it together!" She grabbed an arrow off a table. "Here, go ahead and focus on this." She held it out in front of me.

I felt kind of silly, staring at a solitary arrow, but I did so. I tried to memorize all the lines in the wood and the exact way the tip shown in the light.

"Ready?" she asked, after a minute or so had passed.

I nodded, and she ran to the window, suddenly throwing the arrow outside with a dramatic flourish.

"What are you doing?"

She grinned, shutting the window. "Alright, can you see the arrow?"

"I…" I closed my natural right eye and conjured the image of the arrow I had been staring at moments ago. Suddenly, the eye was lightly pulsing. I could see the arrow now, sitting on a rock down below. On top of that, there was a sort of glowing light calling to me outside the window. Deciding to follow it, I jumped out the window, and even though it was not visible to my natural eye right away, I found the arrow and picked it up.

I brought it back to the training room.

"Very interesting!" Hathor exclaimed. "Isn't that marvelous?"

"I mean…I see how it could be useful in everyday life, or as a party trick, but how would this help me in battle?"

"Hmmmm..." Hathor tapped the table. "Wait, picture this–let's say you're about to go into an unknown area to face enemies, wouldn't being able to see the surroundings before you get there be useful?"

While I couldn't deny the logic, one major issue still remained. It wouldn't help me find Apep. But I wasn't going to tell Hathor that, so I simply said: "I would still like to work on locating people as well," as casually as possible.

She nodded. "Of course, this is just the beginning," she assured me. "We'll go a little longer today, and then I have some studying I'd like you to do before your next session!" I couldn't help but smile.

She seemed to really enjoy the teacher role. Her enthusiasm was infectious due the enthusiasm she had about every little development that we made. I had never heard someone so excited about assigning homework before.

"Read up about previous Eyes of Ra, as well as gods with eye powers in general. Let's explore what those who came before can teach us. We can try out some new ideas next time we meet."

Another good idea, unfortunately. What was Sekhmet going to say when she heard who was training me? Well, she should have taught me herself if that's what she wanted.

I started to walk away, but stopped before I reached the door. "How come you don't use any of your other powers?" I asked, turning around.

"My other powers?"

"Yes, I mean, you aren't a part of the Eyes of Ra anymore...but you're an ancient sky god. But all people see you use are your powers around music, dancing, and putting on parties. Why is that?" I put my hand over my mouth.

What if I had offended her? She might stop teaching me.

I would've told you it was only practical, that I needed someone to work with me on my powers, and she was simply the only choice. But the truth is, I didn't want to hurt her feelings.

But Hathor just laughed. "Well, first off, I am very good at those things. Are you familiar with the sistrum, Bastet?"

I nodded. It was a percussion instrument. It had a curved metal frame and featured rings around it. When rattled, it made a sort of clanging sound that could be soft or loud depending on the makeup of the particular sistrum and the pressure put on it by the player.

"I invented that, in case you weren't aware," she said proudly.

"I...didn't know that." I said, genuinely impressed. The instrument had become a clear part of many religious ceremonies, complementing many pieces of music that had been used for centuries.

"Yes, and I have provided blessings over the years to many artisans who created dances and songs I promise you have encountered before." She shrugged. "I simply find that much more interesting than fighting wars."

"I don't have much interest in fighting wars either," I admitted. Although a fight currently dominated my mind and actions, I was fighting for freedom. I wanted to bless my people, asking for children and protection for their beloved pets.

Perhaps we had more in common than I thought.

"You don't miss it? Being an eye of Ra, being viewed as powerful by others?"

Hathor tilted her head, looking thoughtful. "Not particularly. I am glad it let me meet your father, though."

Perhaps she saw the apprehension in my eyes upon his being mentioned. "I would've been with him earlier, you see, but he wasn't ready."

"Really?" I asked. I had no idea she was interested in my father before she started slowly filtering into his life over the last few years.

"Of course. He loved your mother too much. He needed time. I would never want to disparage her memory," she said, her voice suddenly more serious.

"You tried to fall in love with…others?" I worried again at the inclusion of this question, but the conversation had gone this far.

"I did try," she answered. "And yes, that led to a few entanglements I didn't quite plan. Have you heard of Horus? He was only one of many who made promises he didn't actually plan to keep."

My eyes widened. "Horus is one of the…"

"Fathers of my unclaimed children? Yes, he is Ify's father. But he has no lenwest in being so, and I have no interest in forcing him to do so. My son is strong—he will thrive regardless."

"You do not need to pity me, Bastet," she continued, seeing the look in my eyes. "Horus was not destined to be mine. And it left me free to be with your father. I am well aware of what people say about me."

"Why don't you correct them?" I asked. "That Ify, and your other two children, that it wasn't your intention to not marry? I'm sure it would make a difference for your reputation."

"I don't feel the need to do so," Hathor responded. "For one, there are some who will never believe me, regardless of what I say. And to out my children's fathers puts unwelcome attention and potentially even danger for them. I only care what the people in my life feel about me. Like your father."

My face flushed. Sekhmet had just believed what people said, and therefore, I had to. I had barely pushed back or questioned the narrative we had been fed.

"Thanks for sharing all this with me," I said.

"Of course. I want you and your sister to have a relationship with me. Although I realize with your sister, that might be a bit harder."

I chuckled. "You aren't wrong. She is fiercely protective of my father…But I promise you, she is more than her rough demeanor."

"I believe you," she assured me. "I greatly appreciate how you both care for him. It is a testament to who he is as a man and a father. You both protect him in different ways. And I want to protect him too."

I almost considered telling her my true intentions. That using my powers to slay Apep wouldn't just free Sekhmet and me, Ra would be free to focus on his people, on all he did for Egypt and its gods. He would no longer be at risk of Apep attacks.

But I could guess where her loyalty lay, and it wasn't with me.

12

A DISCOVERY

Someone was waiting for me in the library the next evening.

"Ptah!" I exclaimed, my heart warming at seeing his familiar face. I ran up and hugged him.

"Bastet, it's been days, you've really been worrying me." His eyes watched me, full of concern. "I haven't been able to find you at all, and you ignored my messenger bird…"

I slouched. "Oh, Ptah, I'm sorry, I didn't mean to worry you, things have just been…"

I trailed off, studying the concern in his face. Perhaps it was time to tell him the truth. Wouldn't it feel nice to say it? To share the burden with someone who really knew me, but wasn't as closely involved as my sister. To be able to ask questions out loud, not just in my mind.

And for some reason, the moment he had walked in the door, I had instantly felt safer, my chest a little lighter despite nothing really changing in my environment.

I took a deep breath sund then opened up to him about everything—the prophecy, talking to my sister, even about my powers, a stream of consciousness. I was speaking quickly, the words almost stumbling over each other.

Ptah listened intently, his eyes widening at some points.

"That's heavy," he said once I was done. "Thank you for telling me all this."

"Yes, that is certainly a word for it," I agreed, sitting on top of an empty table, wanting to rest for a moment.

He reached out his hand toward me, and I tilted my head. Was he trying to hold mine? But before it crossed the distance between us, he pulled it back, as if just stretching. "What do you plan to do?"

"I'm trying to figure out what I can do," I said truthfully, gesturing at the books around me.

He glanced at them before saying, "Have you considered finding this Keket your father mentioned? The one the prophecy refers to as the successor?"

I paused. I hadn't. It seemed like a later piece of the puzzle, finding a mysterious daughter of darkness to take over Apep's role once he was eliminated. Truth be told, though, she could be useful. Perhaps she had information about her father we didn't. But would she even support the mission? Father mentioned him, and Amun had grown aware of Socket's powers. But he hadn't said anything about whether they approached it. Was whomever his mother was enough to keep him on the path of light, despite his powers and lineage?

"I'm not sure how to go about it," I said finally.

Ptah looked thoughtful. "There has to be a way to summon her. There is a way to summon every god. We can figure it out together."

I smiled. "Ptah, I really appreciate how supportive you're being," I noted. "My family isn't quite at the same level." Not even close.

It was nice to not be researching alone for once. With my dad's disapproval and my sister's skepticism, I had been looking on my own. I hadn't even felt safe opening up to Henet, since nearly anywhere on the boat, my father would be able to hear.

Ptah smiled softly. "Of course, Bast, we're obviously going to find a way around this prophecy. Maybe Keket can help."

"Around this prophecy?" I asked, suddenly wondering if we were having the same conversation.

"Well… yes, obviously you can't fight Apep. We will find someone who can, so that you can get your freedom."

I lowered my head, not wanting him to see the sadness in my face.

He doesn't believe in me either. I felt my eyes water and quickly rubbed away the moisture.

Ptah put his hand on my shoulder. "You're going to be okay. I promise. I'm not going to let anything happen to you. Don't be scared."

He thought I was just afraid. Why had I assumed he was any different than my family? No one believed in me. Not a single person I had told the whole truth told me I could do it. I felt so foolish.

I swallowed, looking at the floor for a moment longer as I blinked away the tears. "Should… should we see if there are any records of her in here?"

He looked at me for a moment longer, as if there was something else he wanted to say. But then just nodded and started looking through scrolls. For a while, the only sound was the turning of pages. And even though Ptah was with me, I still felt alone.

After another hour of searching, it became clear little was recorded about Keket. Very few records even mentioned her name, and if they did it was often a throw-away line about Apep's life before he was relegated to only living within Duat. This did not surprise me, as I likely would've heard of her existence earlier otherwise.

"This eye power of yours, you said you can only use it on your family?" Ptah inquired.

I put down what I was reading. "I need to have a connection with someone, whether by blood or some…kind of emotional tie."

He opened his mouth, as if to ask something, but then stopped.

At that moment, we both wondered if I was connected enough to Ptah to locate him.

"Since I haven't met Keket, I wouldn't be able to locate her," I continued, breaking the awkward moment.

"Wait…" Ptah turned back to what he was reading, but after only a moment, exclaimed, "This is it!"

"What?"

He brought the scroll he was reading over to me and pointed to a paragraph.

The passage read:

*And upon the fervent prayers of the people
Amun created the scarab staff.*

This staff had one purpose: to be used in a time of great need.

By placing your hand on it, it shall read your lifeblood.

Then, it may summon any god, but an individual may use it only once in their lifetime.

"Wait…I remember this…" I said slowly, closing my eyes and searching my mind for a memory. I started to pace the space between the table where we sat and the shelves, hoping the movement would spark something.

"A couple of years ago…my father was telling us at dinner how he was taking it back from the people because they were abusing it or something…I hadn't been listening closely at the time, as it had been a conversation between him and Sekhmet. "They used it to call on dark gods or ask for inappropriate requests…"

Ptah interlocked his fingers and grinned. "And I've seen where your father has it, because I helped design the space."

I clapped my hands. Of course.

Together we locked eyes and said in unison, "The vaults."

13

VAULTS

The vaults were located on a floor above the living quarters, as far away as possible from prying eyes. They contained a large variety of magical artifacts, most of which were created for my father's court. But, as we had remembered last night, they also contained confiscated goods.

The plan was simple. Ptah would distract the guards, and I would slip into full cat form. This would use most of my *ka*, so I would have to hurry.

I had only seen the vaults once, but I remembered the items were separated by type—amulets, staffs, swords, shields, and the like. I would go straight for the staves and look for a scarab.

After a quick look no one was watching, we went down the hidden door behind my father's throne and walked down the stairs. I stopped behind a pillar once we were within eyesight of the guards. Ptah followed suit. To fit behind the thin marble, we had to stand quite close to each other, my shoulder brushing his.

It made me blush.

Ptah gave me a quick wink, and then he stepped out into their view.

He had never been a good liar, so I was not surprised that he went with something vaguely plausible. "I'm here to do an inspection," he announced.

The guards—two goat half-gods—looked him up and down, recognizing him immediately. They mumbled something to each other. Ptah had garnered decent success over the years thanks to his impressive creations, but he was not their boss —Ra was.

"We haven't heard anything about an inspection, sir," said the one on the right side, fidgeting with a spear. The other one looked past Ptah, but luckily didn't see me.

Ptah stood up straight and puffed out his chest. He deepened his voice. "I created this vault, and it is important that I check that it is structurally sound and there is no way to break in from outside. We wouldn't want intruders getting into Ra's magical artifacts, would we?"

I suppressed the urge to laugh.

"Yasin, you go with him," said the same guard after a moment. "I'll stay here."

I frowned at that. We had hoped to go in alone. But Ptah didn't miss a beat, adjusting. "Several of the doors are quite heavy. I think I'll need both of you."

For a second, I worried they were growing suspicious, as they took a long time to respond.

But finally, Yasin spoke up. "Come on, brother, it will be fine. If someone tries to come in, we will still hear them.

I breathed a sigh of relief. As soon as they turned their backs and started walking in, I closed my eyes, harnessed my magic, and transformed into my cat form.

Ptah led the guards near the back of the vault in his show of "checking for structural integrity".

It always took me a moment to adjust to the shorter height and new perspective of everything when I changed, so I blinked slowly, getting my bearings. The column looked massive now. But as I ran to the door, I enjoyed my enhanced speed.

The touch of my paws on the floor was so soft I didn't need to worry about being heard.

The last time I was here, I certainly hadn't been in this form. *Has it always been so big?*

Lucky for me, the items were kept behind locked bars instead of glass or additional doors—almost like prison cells. The metal bars looked tight, but not too tight that a cat couldn't slip through.

I bounded down the hallway on the right, purely guessing which side to go. I passed the shields and a room full of armor. Near the end of the hallway, I was beginning to wonder if I had gone the wrong way when I finally saw a cell full of staves.

Yes! I slipped through the bars easily, victoriously. My tail twitched in excitement.

Picking things up was harder in this form, and I wished I were looking through amulets instead. I had to use a lot more effort to push through items that would have been light to the touch in my human form. Luckily, some of the staves were small enough to push with my teeth.

It took longer than I would have liked, but I found the Scarab Staff leaning in the corner.

Curses, I thought, upon seeing its size.

My first instinct was that I would have to change back. Carrying it in my mouth would not work, not all the way to the exit. If I had more time, maybe I could roll it down the hallway with my paws. But there is no way Ptah could keep them distracted that long.

In my semi-human form, I wouldn't be able to get back through the bars. Pricking my ears for sound, I desperately looked around the room for a solution.

I noticed a window in the upper-left corner. I knew below us lay a river. Normally, throwing something into it would mean losing it to the deep water.

But if I used my all-seeing eye…

I opened my mouth as wide as I could and clamped down on the Scarab Staff. My grip was tenuous, but good enough to pick it up. I swung around a few times and threw it out the window. It landed awkwardly on the sill, then gravity took over, and it fell out of view.

Hearing footsteps, I bounded out of the cell, down the hallway, and back to the entrance.

I heard one of the guards saying, "Surely you've seen enough?" He sounded annoyed.

"I suppose," Ptah said, looking around, presumably for me. He saw me running and stopped suddenly, distracting the guards. "What's that over there?" He pointed in the opposite direction from where I was headed.

"What?"

"Oh, my mistake, I thought I saw something unlocked. Everything appears to be in order." He coughed awkwardly. "I will tell Ra you are taking good care of the vault."

I continued my way down the stairs, not stopping to transform until I reached the living quarters. When I changed back, I sat down to regain my breath.

Ptah joined me a couple of minutes later. "Did you get it?" he asked, frowning when he saw nothing in my hands.

I explained what I had done with the window and the river.

"Well, that was certainly creative." He laughed. He was well aware I hated swimming. "Do you want me to go for it? You can tell me where to dive."

I shook my head. "I appreciate that, but I don't think I can explain it to someone else. I need to follow the light from the object I'm tracking. But, do you think you could provide backup—just in case? I'll throw the staff up so you can catch it, and I can swim back without carrying it."

"Of course, lead the way. But first, I was impressed with those guards, right?" He puffed out his chest again, and I rolled my eyes.

We made our way to the river flowing along the back side of Ra's temple. The temple was designed so the river surrounded its rear like a partial moat. If you tried to use one of the back entrances, you would have to cross a bridge.

These bridges were usually retracted at night to ward off any surprise visitors.

Anyone could try to swim through the river instead, but the water moved fast, and it was quite cold at night.

"You're sure about this?" Ptah asked, eyeing the current.

"Yes," I assured him. "Wait here. If I'm down too long, come find me. Otherwise…when I throw the staff up, I am on my way back."

"Alright, I will be right here."

I cleared my throat and looked down. From above, the plan seemed more complicated than it had when I had tossed the staff out the window. The tracking light was visible, but it would not help with the general visibility issues of swimming through dark water at night.

Cats and water did not usually mix. But in that water lay my next step toward freedom. I just needed to find it.

Taking the biggest breath I could manage, I plunged in.

I had forgotten I would not be alone in the river. Fish swam around me, and rocks and weeds coated the bottom. I did my best to focus only on the light that would lead me to the staff.

It felt much longer than the one minute it took me to reach the flat rock where the staff rested. I was grateful it wasn't buried under stones. Some fish parted at my approach.

The moment I got it in my hands, I paddled for air. When I surfaced, I gasped, the chill hitting my face.

"That…was not fun," I yelled to Ptah, before throwing the staff toward him.

He caught it before it hit the ground. "Great job! Now, let's get you out of here before your father's guards get suspicious."

As I started to swim back to shore, I realized my father might routinely take inventory of the vaults. Would he notice the staff was missing? I would have to come up with a way to put it back later, though sneaking in a second time didn't feel viable.

I shook my head. Not the time to worry about that. I needed to get to land.

But when I tried to swim, I suddenly couldn't move. My ankle didn't budge. I tried to look, but the water was too dark. Seaweed, maybe?

I thrashed—probably not helpful. I was close enough to the surface to snatch a breath, but then I was yanked back down as a plant pulled on my ankle.

"BASTET?" Ptah was yelling, but I barely heard him.

I was too focused on catching my breath to call for help. Each push took more effort. My limbs ached, growing tired. I stayed under longer each time.

I heard a loud splash. A blurry image of Ptah jumping in was the last thing I saw before I closed my eyes.

What I assume was a few minutes later, I woke up to him leaning in to give me mouth-to-mouth. He stopped with his lips less than an inch from mine. "I'm—I'm good…" I said, feeling mortified.

Ptah backed away quickly, his face turning red. "Oh, I'm glad, I was just…it didn't seem like you were breathing at first. You weren't responding when I shook you. I got scared, so I was going to…"

Still breathing heavily, and grateful to be on land, "I understand," I assured him, shaking off some of my fur. "I…I would've done the same thing."

He took off his jacket and wrapped it around me. "I'm just so glad you're alright. You honestly scared me for a moment there, Bast."

"The great daughter of Ra, taken out by some seaweed…" I joked, pulling the fabric tighter as I shivered.

"Don't even," Ptah said sternly, though relief softened his face.

We sat there for a moment. Then I looked up at him, the realization of what he had done finally hitting me. "You saved my life."

He shrugged. "Like you said, you would've done the same thing for me."

I wanted to say more, explain to him how much I appreciated it. But I could not find the words.

He handed me the Scarab Staff, shaking off the water. "So when are we doing this?" He looked up at the sky. "I don't think we have much time until dawn…"

I rubbed my hands over the red scarab at the top of the staff. "Tomorrow. And I feel a bit… rude, asking this after all you've done, but would it be okay if I go alone?"

Ptah frowned. "What if she's dangerous? We are hopeful of her allegiance based on the prophecy and your father's words, but we didn't find any confirmation."

"I just think this conversation should be from ancient god daughter to ancient god daughter…if that makes sense."

"Alright…" he said, sounding hesitant. "But try not to do anything reckless?"

"Sure, sure," I said with a hand wave as we walked back to the palace. "By the way. I am curious…have you ever helped someone breathe before? Using that mouth-to-mouth thing you were attempting?"

I glanced at his lips for a moment before quickly looking away, wondering what they would feel like.

Why am I thinking about that?

He was blushing again. "Well, no, but there's a first time for everything."

14

KEKET

The first thing that struck me about Keket was how small she was. The goddess had a green snake's head, clearly inherited from her father, but she did not carry the same threatening aura.

She stood a foot shorter than I. Her large blue eyes made her appear younger than she was. She did not carry herself like her mother, but I could see Tawaret's facial features in the slope of her nose and size of her ears.

"Thank you for answering my call," I said, choosing my words carefully. I wasn't sure where her alliances lay. As far as I was aware, she did not attend any of the festivals. Sekhmet had certainly never met her.

Keket seemed nervous, looking all over the room instead of making eye contact. "Yes, I am here," she muttered.

I couldn't judge her reaction; a magical artifact had never summoned me myself.

"I am not sure what you have been told," I continued. "I assume your mother mentioned our meeting."

Keket finally looked at me, only for a moment. "You want to talk about my f-father," she responded, stuttering.

"If you are comfortable doing so…please, sit."

She stayed standing. "He doesn't talk to me, if that's what you're asking…" She flicked her tongue in and out—a calming habit, perhaps.

"No, I didn't assume he would," I assured her. "However, as his child, you are of course… connected."

"Unfortunately."

That seems promising. "I am sure you are aware, but I serve as defense for my father from yours."

"Because of the curse," she replied.

She seemed to know more about me than I knew about her.

"Yes, it binds Sekhmet and me to our nighttime duties and daytime slumber. I am looking to break that by fighting him."

Keket jumped suddenly, which was a bit unsettling. "You're insane!"

If she didn't sound so scared, this might have offended me. "I don't think that's really your place to say," I replied. "I want my sister and me to be free, and this is the only way."

"I'm not helping you fight him." She shook her head repeatedly.

"I'm not asking you to," I assured her. "I am here to speak with you about afterward."

"After?"

"After I defeat him. Despite everything, your father serves a purpose in the natural order of the world. When daytime ends, he releases darkness into the sky and gives the Earth a reprieve from light. When he is…removed, someone else will need to step into that role." I felt strange using the word to his daughter, even though I was being open with my intentions.

Keket let out a breathy, shocked laugh. "Step into that role…"

"My understanding from my father is that you are capable." I was beginning to doubt that, however.

"I have night powers," she confirmed. "But you speak of a reality that will never come to be. But I was born there…it's full of demons and darkness. Nothing but demons and darkness. My mother barely got me out."

"Do you mean his lair? Do you know where it is?" I asked. If she could tell me, I wouldn't need to use my eye.

"No, I was still a baby when we left. I tell you this so you might abandon this madness."

I started to lose patience. "Listen, I told you, I want to be free and—"

"And if I help you, I might get cursed too."

"I'm not asking you to fight," I repeated. I had secretly planned to ask her about any weaknesses of serpent gods, but that seemed futile now. "Once again, I just want to ensure you are ready to step into your role as keeper of the night once he is gone."

"I don't think you fully understand what you are asking of me." Her tone slowly shifted from scared to angry. "I have done everything I can to distance myself from him. To remain on the path of good, and convince everyone who sees my face that it is not his.

"I will forever be in his shadow," she explained. "If I take his place, who says I won't become him? Mad in that forever darkness?"

"Do you not believe you control your own destiny?" I asked, confused.

She didn't answer, so I pulled out the prophecy. "Or, if you don't want to believe in your own destiny—listen to this."

I let the prophecy play, watching Keket's face, particularly during the closing lines.

"This must be what Thoth has been trying to get me to read. I never open his scrolls."

I had wondered if either he or my father had approached her. My father felt we had hit a wall, but I doubted the god of knowledge would write off his own prophecy. It frustrated me to realize the answers I had been desperately seeking had literally been mailed to her—and she ignored them.

"Do you see why I have come to you now?" I pointed to the parchment as it settled on the table. "My efforts will be for naught if there is no one to manage the night sky. You are just as much a part of this future as I am. The world needs you."

"I see why you have come to me." Her voice fell to almost a whisper. "I just wish you hadn't."

"Because you can't say no to saving the world?" I asked, hopeful.

"I'd certainly like to, but...I will speak with my mother. That is the most I can offer. If she truly believes she can train me in the way of the skies...I will consider this..."

"When is your coming of age?" I asked, referencing the last line. "I am about to have my birthday, but it seems like we are beholden to yours, not mine."

"It is not for several months. Therefore, you must give me time."

It seemed the best I was going to get. I accompanied her to the exit, promising to keep her updated.

"Actually, how can I contact you?" I asked. "This staff is for one-time use. Would you provide me with your location?"

"That is a secret few have heard, Bastet. I don't have any interest in changing that. How can you prove you won't tell anyone else?"

"Because your safety is of great importance, should I succeed," I assured her. "That prophecy you just heard, I intend to bring it to pass, no matter what it takes."

"Fetch me some parchment."

I ran to do so before she could change her mind, handing her a reed pen as well. "I promise you will not regret this."

Keket handed me the paper and pen back. "Only reach out when you are sure. I will provide you with my answer only then."

As I watched her leave, I couldn't help feeling grateful for my father. Yes, he was resistant now. But because of how he raised me, I had always believed in myself. I was empowered to take on my role as a defender of the sun. If tragedy were to strike, I would be proud to represent him.

I was not Apep's only victim. And I was going to fight for all of them.

The next day in the library, I slammed a book closed. Yet another one with nothing useful in it.

I could see the outline of a battle plan—a rough sketch at least. I had unlocked my powers, begun training, and lined up Apep's successor. But it would not be enough to convince Sekhmet. First, I still hadn't located Apep's lair.

But more than that, I needed a weapon. I loved my trusty spear, but I needed something blessed by the ancient gods that would truly give us the advantage. So I returned to the library and tore through books and scrolls, only stopping when dawn approached.

Unsurprisingly, most gods kept their most powerful weapons in their possession. Even if I could get a hold of it somehow, my father's sun scepter would be of no use. While the *Wascepter*, originally used by Set, was impressive, it only worked for those who could imbue magic into it.

I was about to give up for the night when I found the story of Neith's Khopesh.

Neith was one of the original goddesses. As humans and gods alike went to war, she discovered the power to create weapons that could turn the tide of battles. Believing her weapons to be too deadly, she locked them away in enchanted chests hidden throughout the world.

Suddenly, I remembered something I had seen in the records of past failed attempts to fight Apep, and I quickly shuffled through the papers.

There it was, a record made by a priest named Malik:

As conventional weapons continue to bring us nothing but ruin, we must look to the celestial for answers. A disciple of mine came with a bold claim—that he has located the Khopesh created by Neith and locked away long ago. He says he has convened with the war god and explained our plight, but she said she will not interfere with the wars of the gods. But she did reveal the sword's location. I will record the coordinates for posterity, but I do not want to risk more lives than I already have on such a venture.

Attached was a picture of Neith's Khopesh. It was a combination of a sword and a sickle. At the end was a snake around an ankh—a cross with a curved end that was prominent on many of the ancient gods' weapons.

What better weapon to kill a snake than one featuring a snake? Any fatigue from poring over the texts faded, replaced by excitement.

I brushed through the papers and found a map I had studied earlier. I set it down beside the record and used my finger to trace the coordinates. When it landed, I grinned. Lake Nassor! That was a sight I recognized. I hadn't expected to be familiar with the weapon's location.

I had my powers; I had met with our enemy's successors, and now, I'd found a weapon. It was time to arrange a meeting with my sister.

15

BIRTHDAY

The next day was Sekhmet's and my birthday—a day I usually looked forward to. It was one of the rare times that all of us ate together as a family. Shu even brought his wife, Tefnut. I usually brought Ptah, and Sekhmet often invited one of her war god friends, such as Montu.

But this year, it felt strange. For one, I didn't know what to expect from my father.

And second, this birthday marked what was supposed to be the start of us unlocking our full powers. Because of our curse, it couldn't be that— it would just be a nice dinner and some cake.

Yes, Heka had unlocked one of my powers, but I had not unlocked my full potential by any means. I appreciated the progress I had made with Hathor. But my strength and speed were still capped, as well as the light powers I would eventually receive.

Everyone but Father had arrived when I sat down next to Ptah.

"Happy birthday!" he said, smiling at me as I sat down.

I smiled back, but it was halfhearted.

Because of his unique self-creation Ptah had not had to grow into his powers. He couldn't fully understand the emotions I was dealing with.

"Took your time," Sekhmet remarked. But she was smiling, so she couldn't be that annoyed with me. Probably the wine in front of her.

Tefnut was a fellow cat deity of the leopard variety—so much so that people had joked she looked like she was already a part of the family even before she joined it by marrying my brother. But she certainly wasn't—she had a nice, still-living mother.

"Good to see you again," she said in greeting, which I returned.

A few moments later, my father came in. He didn't meet my gaze.

He did not enter alone—Hathor stood by his side. I shot a look at Sekhmet, who started frowning. Checking the others' reaction, Ptah just raised an eyebrow. Shu and Tefnut, however, did not seem surprised. *Do they know something I don't?* Hathor certainly hadn't mentioned anything to me in our training.

"Hello all. It is good to see my family together," my father said. He beckoned a servant to bring out the food.

"Yes, it's always good to see family and loved ones," Sekhmet remarked, shooting Hathor a look.

If she sensed her animosity, my father's plus one did not show it. "I'm so glad I'm here to celebrate with you!"

The awkwardness dissipated as Shu and my father began conversing about something, and the servants brought out the food.

It was quite impressive—plates piled with several kinds of fish, fresh figs, and many sides.

I'm not sure I could even name all the vegetable options. The smells were so good, I could almost close my eyes and forget my worries.

But nothing was ever that simple.

For one thing, what if someone noticed my amulet was missing? I wore a scarf to cover my neck, but it was thin and almost transparent.

"So, any news on your part?" I asked Tefnut, trying to make polite conversation.

She regaled me with a story of my nephew, Geb, who had recently started talking. She loved being a mother.

It was something I had thought about, of course. While immortal deities did not die of age, they still could die unnatural deaths. The world of gods was not always safe. Similar to what I understood of mortals, we wanted to pass on our legacy. But it was one of many things I could not fully wrap my mind around until Apep was slain.

Misreading the look on my face, Tefnut suddenly stopped talking. "Oh, I won't bore you with tales of motherhood." She laughed. "What is new with you?"

I didn't think I could provide an answer for that. "Oh, nothing too…"

Hathor suddenly jumped in from the other side of the table. "I think you're keeping busy, wouldn't you say?" She winked at me.

I could feel Sekhmet's stare drilling into me. Wonderful, I would have to explain that later. I had already been planning to meet with her and Ptah after my research, but now it would look like I was hiding something.

Luckily, my father chose that moment to stand up and give his customary toast.

"Each year on this day, I remember when Amun approached me and offered to provide me with two daughters who would represent two halves of my life, my dedication to the sun and its people"—he pointed his glass toward me—"and my fighting spirit and power that I use to protect the people of Egypt." He pointed it at Sekhmet now.

I recognized the speech. Normally, he moved on to the part where he talked about the future we would one day have. But suddenly, he went off-script.

"I never imagined I'd be raising you two alone." His voice choked up a bit.

I looked over at Sekhmet, whose mouth was wide open. It had been one thing for him to mention her when we were alone, and discussing the prophecy. But in front of others? I couldn't remember the last time that happened.

"Shu, you know—he was grown up before she was taken from us, and I'm so glad he got to have that…"

Shu was clearly surprised, too, by the mention of our mother, his eyes going cloudy. Tefnut grabbed his hand.

"No one could replace your mother," he continued. "But I like to believe from the fields of the gods she is watching us, even now, and that she would want this family to grow and be happy. That's why…I'm so happy to tell you I have asked Hathor to be my wife, and she has said yes."

Tefnut clapped, which was probably for the best, as no one else had a normal reaction. Shu still seemed in shock at the mention of our mother. I froze in place with a napkin half lifted, and Sekhmet well…she dropped her glass, which shattered.

"You'll never replace her," she hissed, before getting up and walking out the door.

"Sekhmet, wait!" my father called out as she left. He started to stand up.

I shook my head. "No, let me do it. Please."

I got up and chased her down the hall. She stopped at the end before turning to face me.

"What, Bastet? Are you here to tell me to play nice? To let our father marry some scheming goddess that is clearly only with him for the status? She can plan all the parties she wants from this giant temple!" She threw her hands up.

"I think you misunderstand her a little," I said, slowly approaching her. "She's not…like that. Other gods used her and lied to her, but that's not her fault…"

"And why do you know so much about her anyway?" she snapped. "What, are you friends now or something?"https://www.youtube.com/watch?v=OHBNdj_n0Tc

"No, listen—she's been helping me with something. I was literally getting ready to tell you and Ptah tonight that I wanted to meet, to discuss the plan, and it will all make sense if you can just be patient."

"You went to *Hathor* for help?" Wonderful, she sounded angrier.

"It's… Please just meet me tomorrow night. And give me a chance to explain?" I pleaded.

"Fine, but I'm not going back in there."

"That's…sure, if that's really what you want. I'll just eat your part of the cake."

Sekhmet rolled her eyes and walked away.

I tried to come up with a good excuse for my sister as I headed back. But was there really anything believable? She hadn't exactly left quietly.

My father looked a bit glum when I returned alone.

"Your sister wasn't interested in returning?" he asked.

I shook my head. "She just needs time to cool off," I replied, deciding being honest was the easiest option. I turned to Hathor. "I apologize on her behalf."

"I appreciate that," Hathor said softly. "I'm sure she will come around eventually."

"Well, I will have to give Sekhmet her present later," my father said. When I looked into his eyes, I did not see anger. Something had softened him lately. Was it Hathor, the plan to marry again, that brought on this change?

Could it be because of me? He did seem to have to regret his many secrets. Perhaps he thought that if he was nice and accommodating, I would be less likely to go off and fight a battle he did not believe I could win.

He had no way to guess, of course, that I had just conspired with my sister to meet about that very thing the next evening. I probably shouldn't get used to this side of him. I didn't anticipate the same softness in his eyes when he found out.

He brought over a small parcel and set it by my plate. "Well…you can open yours, at least."

Before opening it, I primed myself to respond well. My father, like many men, did not always choose the best gifts for us. We'd received strangely designed scarves, hair pieces, and other accessories over the years. We weren't even quite sure where he found things, so out of the common fashion—he might have had them custom-made.

But what was inside was beautiful. It was a golden bracelet, encrusted with opals, with the familiar ankh symbol of life as the central design, carved out of a white metal. "Is this…?"

"Your mother had these made when you were born. If you open the ankh, you will see it contains a vial of holy Nile water. She imbued it with powerful healing properties. She wanted a bit of her blessings to be with you, even when you were far away." His voice choked. "And even when the vial is gone, I hope it reminds you of her all the same."

"It's beautiful," I breathed.

"Yes, she meant for it to be given on this birthday, the one in which you two reach adulthood. She recognized even then that the life of daughters of Ra would not be one without danger."

"I have one too," Shu chimed in. "Well, actually, mine was an anklet, which is more befitting of a man, in my opinion."

I laughed, letting Ptah help me with the clasp of the bracelet. "Thank you, Father. I am glad you waited until this birthday to bestow it."

"I am grateful she left something for this day," he agreed. "She looks out for us always, I truly believe that."

The servants walked in with cake at that point, breaking up the heaviness. Despite teasing Sekhmet about eating her portion, I set some aside for her.

Eventually, people began to clear out, and it was just Ptah and me left at the table.

"Well, that was a birthday dinner for the books, wasn't it?" I asked Ptah once we were alone.

"Things are never boring when your sister is around, that's for sure," he replied, laughing. "You seem alright with it though—Hathor and your father?"

I took the final sip left in my goblet, considering my answer. "I suppose I am. The idea was a bit strange at first, but…being with her seems to make him happy. Isn't that what we all want in life? Someone who makes us happy?"

"Yes, I believe that's what they say."

"Regardless, his giving us these bracelets—and the emotion he showed—proves that he will always honor her place where it matters." I ran my hand over the smooth metal.

"Yes, it's quite a hard gift to follow, I can tell you that," Ptah remarked.

"Oh, you got me something? Really?" I put my hand on my heart, touched.

He shrugged. "It's your eighteenth birthday, of course, I got you something."

He pulled out a parcel, painstakingly wrapped in bamboo paper.

Ptah often did something for my birthday—sometimes he cooked me something. When we were kids, I once got a "credit" to choose what we did for the day. Usually, it was something along those lines—an experience or consumable item. This was the first time he had given me a tangible gift.

I opened it slowly, respecting the time the wrapping job must have taken.

Inside was a set of paint brushes. The handle was made out of smooth maple. Each was carved to perfectly fit the grip of my hand, clearly designed for me. Small sun symbols were etched along them. The most interesting part, though, was the bristles.

Each brush used different materials—some thick, some soft to the touch. All of them glowed. The effect was subtle—easier to see in a darker room—but undeniable.

He watched me intently, clearly nervous.

"They're beautiful," I breathed, running my fingers over the brushes. I could tell the quality was impressive.

He smiled. "The glow, it's magic I imbued into the bristles. It will make anything you paint glow on the canvas as well. I figured you would like it for painting suns or even stars."

It was so thoughtful—of course it was. Ptah knew me as well as any member of my family, maybe more. I placed my hand on top of his for a moment. "Thank you."

He shrugged, but a giant smile spread across his lips. "Of course, Bast."

I didn't want the night to end. Despite Sekhmet's spectacle and the tension between father and me, it had been a much better night than I expected. I wanted to sit and talk more, or go with Ptah and paint somewhere with my new brushes.

But, as always, hints of dawn began to appear outside, so I had to excuse myself.

"Will you meet with Sekhmet and me tomorrow night?" I asked, preparing to leave.

"Sure, what's the plan?" Ptah seemed curious.

I gave him a meaningful look—hoping it communicated what I wanted. "I found something quite interesting in the library," I decided to say.

Realization hit him, and he nodded. "Yes, tomorrow night sounds good."

He had saved my life, given me an amazing birthday gift, and was helping me earn my freedom. Emotion welled up, and I kissed him on the cheek. Too nervous to see his reaction, I quickly ran away.

As I headed to my bedroom, I fidgeted with my new bracelet. Curious about the vial inside, I tried to open the ankh. It did not open with a snap or respond to any kind of pressure. There was a very small hole. Did it need some kind of key?

I grew quite tired and barely made it to my bed before closing my eyes. It would have to be a mystery for another day.

16

LAKE NASSOR

The next evening, the three of us met in Sekhmet's war room. I had a lot of information to impart, and I was not sure how it would be received. As they sat down, I took a deep breath and tightened my grip on the documents I had brought.

"I asked you here to catch up on my efforts to break our curse and defeat Apep. Sekhmet," I said, turning to her. "I respect your desire for an actionable plan and to be adequately prepared before you provide combat training and consider joining me. Ptah has been a bit more involved, so he has heard some of this already…but to catch you up…well, first off, I met with Heka."

"And why would you do that?" Sekhmet asked, raising an eyebrow.

"Well, I know my combat skills could only go so far compared to your years of training. But I found a record in the library of a time Heka intervened to help a half-god release his full power."

"And he agreed to help?" she questioned. "Interesting. I did not think he would want to get involved in this sort of thing."

Was she impressed? I stood a little higher. "Yes, he did."

"What did you offer to summon him?" Ptah asked, frowning.

I touched my neck where the amulet used to sit, and Sekhmet groaned.

"Sister, what were you thinking? Father will be furious when he notices. I can't believe he didn't last night, it's not like you had the darkness to hide you."

I shrugged. "It was the only equivalent exchange for what I was asking." I did feel guilty —not that I would admit that. But if I could go back, I would do it again. I had nothing else of comparable magical value.

She shook her head, but curiosity got the best of her. "Alright, well, tell us, what's your power?"

"Well... It's unfortunately not the most... combat-related," I said slowly. But if I wanted her to take me seriously, I needed to sell it better. "I have an all-seeing eye."

"Which means...?"

"It means I can find people," I explained what Heka had told me about how the powers work, and how it might help us find Apep.

"Hmm..." Sekhmet looked thoughtful, luckily not disappointed. "Yes, it's not directly combat-related, but at least finding his location is taken care of...and we could do something with this. Seeing moves of an enemy behind you, perhaps. Give me some lenmore time to think— there's something here..."

"Sure," I replied, still surprised by her reaction. I decided not to tell her I hadn't been able to locate anyone outside of our family and objects yet. I wanted to go there. And if anyone could find a more practical use for the eye, it would be her.

"And I've been training," I continued.

"You told someone else about our efforts?" Sekhmet hissed.

I shook my head. "No, I haven't told her any details...but remember last night when I said I would make things make sense today? Well, this training I've been doing...it's with Hathor."

She frowned.

"How is she as a teacher?" Ptah asked.

"Honestly—better than I thought," I admitted. "She used to have Eye of Ra powers, too, so she had some useful insight. Heka was the one who recommended it."

"And what has she taught you to do with it?" Sekhmet asked, skeptical.

I detailed our training sessions—how I could use items to scout ahead—and even Ptah's and my adventure with the staff, although I left out the parts of me almost drowning and our awkward encounter.

"And...if you're still worried about me in combat, I actually had a proposition," I finished.

Sekhmet's cat ears perked up.

"I am sure you are familiar with Neith's Khopesh?" I saw signs of recognition on their faces. "Ptah, you have seen I have been doing some research in the library. You even helped, which I appreciate. One thing I discovered was that Father's priests found its location. They just didn't feel confident retrieving it."

"Where?" Ptah said. "That is impressive on their part…but what does this have to do with you?"

I turned to him. "When I came across it, I was hoping you might be able to help…it's at Lake Nassor, the one you designed."

"Where Amitt's crocodiles reside?" Sekhmet gasped.

Amitt was a feared hybrid deity made up of a mix of hippopotamus, lion, and crocodile. Many viewed her as a demon, though she was not. She devoured wicked souls. When Anubis judged the dead, he sent wicked souls to Amitt. The souls gave her immense power, but she did not grant prayers.

It was true that Amitt had taken the lake as part of her territory. She supercharged the crocodiles there with piercing teeth and deadly force. I was unsure why she hadn't taken the Khopesh herself. She likely felt she did not need it, but did not want any enemies to gain access either. Many half-gods, in particular, wanted to avenge dead mortal loved ones she had taken.

I nodded, trying to gauge Ptah's reaction, but his face was blank. "They've carved tunnels as dens. I was hoping Ptah could tell us the best places to enter and strike." I told them about the location of the Khopesh in the enchanted chest.

Sekhmet frowned. "This is a dangerous suggestion. I understand why you desire the weapon, but…"

What can I say to convince her? Perhaps flattery would work. "You wisely asked me to come up with a plan. Following your guidance, I sought out my power, worked on setting up Apep's successor, and discovered this weapon. Getting the Khopesh is the final piece of the puzzle."

She furrowed her brow. "When do you want to do this?"

"As soon as possible," I replied.

"Why are you in such a hurry?" Ptah's voice had a strange sharpness.

"Because I should have done this much sooner," I replied firmly.

"But you just opened this conversation with your father less than a fortnight ago. You don't think that we could spend some more time looking for solutions?" His voice was getting louder. "Isn't this daughter a year younger than you, giving us plenty of time?"

I refused to relent. "You mean Keket? Like I said a second ago, I spoke with her. She is considering stepping up should we clear the way, but I promise you she is the farthest thing from a fighter. She is terrified of him."

"Yes, and you should be terrified too," he retorted.

"I don't understand this reaction. Weren't you also hoping for me to finally be free of this ghost of a life?" My jaw clenched.

"I wanted you to ask your father, the second most powerful god of Egypt, to intervene or find a solution. I didn't want you to get yourself killed." I'd never heard him use that tone with anyone, let alone me.

"You don't think I can do it?" I snapped. "Sekhmet will be with me; I'm not going alone."

"Bastet, you don't even have combat power. I'm sorry, but you think you can take the god of chaos with her spears and your…magic eye?"

My nostrils flared. "Whether you think I'm capable or not, I'm prophesied to do it, so my stupid magic eye must be enough."

"You are prophesied to be the one who can kill him, but you are also prophesied to die if you fail," he insisted, drawing out the words slowly.

"Better to die in valor than live half a life," I retorted.

"Really, there's nothing you have right now that's worth living for?" His voice didn't sound angry anymore; it was strained with another emotion—sadness.

I was so tired of the word if. If I became a goddess, if I failed.

Why did no one believe I could succeed? Why did everyone want me to be content with a few hours a day? It was so easy for them to talk about something they could never understand with infinite time at their disposal and powers to wield.

"That's not what I said," I kept my voice firm, but calm.

Clearly, my attempt to diffuse the situation didn't work, because suddenly, Ptah stood up. "How can you be so naive? Do you really think that just because you've read some prophecy and met the god of magic, you're ready to take on the most powerful evil force in our world?"

He did not wait for me to respond. "Actually, why am I doing this…clearly this is going nowhere!"

"That's it? You're just going to leave?" I yelled, but he was already at the door; he didn't look behind to reply as he left and slammed it. The sound reverberated in the now silent room.

"For someone with an enhanced eye, you're quite blind," Sekhmet said after the echo faded.

"What?" I had forgotten she was still there.

"Sister, surely you've realized Ptah is madly in love with you."

"That's insanity," I scoffed.

She rolled her eyes. "You've never noticed him casually hanging around in the middle of the night after you get back from Duat? You think he always has real meetings with Father or needs to 'study blueprints'?"

"That doesn't mean he loves me," I insisted. "We've been friends since forever, that's it." I bit my lip, my thoughts carrying me back to our recent close encounters and the butterflies in my chest when I stood close to him. I didn't feel that with Henet.

But that was a recent development.

"Have you heard of any other god who has remained single for this long?" she continued. "It's not even that he hasn't chosen a wife; Ptah has never even had a lover or consort."

"Neither have we."

Sekhmet chuckled slightly. "I wouldn't make assumptions, Bastet. I am blessed with a bit more free time than you, sister."

I had no idea how to respond to that.

"Either way, if you really have been in the dark about his feelings, now you are not. Do what you like with it—none of my business." She shrugged. "But if you don't go after him, you might lose him forever. And don't tell him I said this, but that would be a shame."

What was I supposed to do with this information? Especially now that he was angry. I wanted to move past this, go back to the way things were. Hadn't enough changed in my life recently?

Restless energy surged through me, and I stood up.

I can't worry about this now.

"I appreciate your insights. Now, I must go."

My heart was beating faster than expected, but not because of the danger. The words of Ptah, Sekhmet, my father, kept reverberating in my brain: "You'll get yourself killed…" "Isn't this enough?"

I would prove them wrong, and it would start with the Khopesh close to.

Lake Nassor was not far from Heliopolis. I remembered when Ptah designed it. It had been one of those glorious sunny evenings where I felt free, not trapped. I loved seeing what Ptah created, especially when he showed me first. There was something special about witnessing a feat of nature before it was revealed to the world.

My dark vision was the only reason I could see anything as I approached. No moonlight or stars could illuminate the shore thanks to the thick reeds and large surrounding trees.

I stopped when I could hear the ripples of water and the frogs trilling. I took refuge behind a tree; crocodiles also had night vision.

If no one would help me fight for my freedom, I'd do it myself.

Wanting eyes on the chest before entering, I picked up a rock and memorized its image, cementing it in my mind. As I threw it into the lake, I moved to a different tree in case the crocodiles awoke. The stone was small, and I heard no movement.

I closed my natural eye and used my magical one to locate the stone. It was slowly sinking to the ground. With practice, I had gotten better at expanding an image past its initial focus. A couple of feet away from where the stone finally rested, I saw the chest. Vines covered it, held down by larger rocks. But I had found it!

Gripping my spear tightly, I peered around the tree and took a step. The ground was not as smooth as I'd expected. I stopped myself from slipping, barely. I took a deep breath and stepped again.

All went well until I got close to the water. I had chosen a spot with no crocodiles nearby. The idea of swimming again did not excite me, considering my experience retrieving the staff. No one was around to save me this time should I drown.

This is how you show them.

I should've looked down. As I took the last step to the edge of the water, my left foot crushed a stick. It made a noise, but I hoped it would not stand out against the sound of the waves lapping the shore or the frogs croaking.

Surely that was not enough to wake them?

First, I saw only one. It made eye contact with me, sizing me up. I raised my spear, my intentions clear. The crocodile's nostrils flared, and I wondered if it could smell my fear.

Then, as if synchronized together, they all woke up. I could see nearly a dozen of them. They did not seem fast, but they outnumbered me. I tried to leap over one and ran to a tree, climbing to the highest branch.

Can crocodiles climb trees? Why hadn't I done more research before I went out? My whole body tensed as I tried to grab hold on to the trunk of the tree for support.

Well, these ones certainly could. Time seemed to slow down, as if my brain wanted to offer me an extra moment before the end. Regret filled every fiber of my being. Even greater was the realization: they were right. All of them.

I couldn't even handle some magic crocodiles. What chance did I have against my father's greatest foe?

If this was the end, I did not want to stare into the dark eyes of the crocodiles. I wanted my last view to be more pleasant. I closed my eyes, and with my all-seeing eye, summoned Ptah's face to my mind.

Before I could see him, everything went dark.

17

AFTERMATH

A breeze carried me several feet away, out of the trees, to where my brother and sister were waiting. Both appeared out of breath.

"Are you alright?" Shu asked, grabbing me and checking for bruises or signs of injury.

"I'm…I'm fine," I said slowly, still coming to terms with the fact I wasn't dead.

"What were you *THINKING*?" Shu yelled, his tone changing instantly.

"I told you she's lost her mind," Sekhmet remarked. I couldn't even blame her. "Now let's get out of here before the crocodiles decide eating us is worth leaving their lake, yes?"

We ran in silence for half a mile until we could see the edges of town. I had never been so grateful to see the paved road and torches lining the path. I often resented that I didn't have time to explore places away from Heliopolis. But at that moment, I simply felt gratitude that I got to see it again.

Shu began pacing. "Sekhmet let me in on this insanity you've been partaking in. I thought you were smarter than this. What is our father going to say?"

"Please don't tell him," I pleaded. Any approval he had given to my research would

149

evaporate instantly. On top of that, he'd likely confine me to my living quarters when not in Duat for months.

"Well, it's clear you need more supervision, and I certainly can't do it," he replied. "I have a child of my own to worry about."

I bristled at the term child, but I was in no place to push back. So instead I just said, "What I did was stupid. I realize that now."

"At least she admits it," Sekhmet noted. She seemed almost amused, which infuriated me.

"You didn't think it was stupid when I first approached you about all this," I pointed out. "You asked me to make a plan. Then you and Ptah decided not to support it."

She snorted. "I never even got to say anything about your plan, Bastet. You just walked out to pull whatever this stunt was."

"Sister," Shu said, his voice pained. "Can you understand how worried we were?"

"Even Sekhmet?" I muttered, still annoyed with her tone.

"Yes, even me."

The sudden softness in her voice shocked me. My brother kept nothing in. He'd tell anyone if he loved or hated them without thinking twice. But Sekhmet was different. I understood logically she loved me; we were bonded together in our plight in a way no outsiders could ever understand. But she was not the type to say it.

Guilt washed over me. Why am I so selfish? Just because they weren't backing my plan didn't mean they didn't care.

Tears filled my eyes. "I'm sorry, Shu. I'm sorry, Sekhmet. I…"

Sekhmet placed her hand on my shoulder—the closest to a hug she had given me since we were children. "I understand."

"You're alright, that's what matters," Shu agreed.

But I couldn't stop crying now. "It should be you," I told Sekhmet.

"What?"

"Thoth's prophecy—he got it wrong. It's clear you should be the chosen one. You're better trained than me. *You* know how to fight. *You* would never rush into a lake of crocodiles with a useless old spear." I threw it into the sand.

"Sister…" Sekhmet said quietly. "Others determined the roles we would serve in this world before we were even born. Our whole lives, we have honored these assignments. This prophecy simply brought to light the fact that in order to be free, something had to change. Clearly, it was always you should end this fight."

I blinked away the moisture from my eyes. "I'm doing this all wrong though, aren't I? Rushing it?"

"I think you should slow down," she replied. "But you have to decide that for yourself."

I nodded. "I'll…I'll do it. I can't wait forever, but there is still time before the deadline…I don't have to do this now."

Shu breathed a sigh of relief. "I am so grateful you have seen sense. If you swear to me this nonsense is over, I will not tell Father."

"Really?" I hadn't thought there was any way to talk him out of it. "I swear—I'll sign in blood if you need me to, no more stupid nonsense.

He laughed. "That won't be necessary. Go get some sleep, both of you."

I was grateful for a fairly quiet night in Duat. Not only was I hiding exhaustion from my near brush with death, but I also desperately wanted space to think. Ptah was not the first person to call me naïve. Sekhmet surely had many times over the years, and our father had implied similar ideas.

Why did it hurt more coming from him? They were the same words.

As I stared off into the dark, I felt my shoulders slump. Perhaps they were right, all of them. Who was I to defeat the god of chaos?

And then there was the fact that my best friend was in love with me.

"Bastet, is everything alright?" Henet walked up to me.

I wished I hadn't been hiding so much from her lately. It was nice to have something I could speak about freely. Leaving out the context of the nature of the fight, I told her how he had stormed out and what Sekhmet had said.

Henet gasped. "How did I not see that coming?" She did not pry into the details of the fight, which I was grateful for. She did, however, ask me the question I had been wrestling with myself. "Do you think you love him?"

I sighed, staring out at the water. "I don't know, it's not something I've ever thought of before."

"Being in love with him?" She tilted her head.

"Being in love at all," I clarified. "My strict curfew hasn't given me a lot of time to think about dates." I realized I had someone more experienced in the ways of the world in front of me. I glanced in her direction. "What has it been like for you?" I asked.

She laughed, covering her mouth with her hand. "I can promise you I have never been in love. I have had…trysts, strange moments. My parents have even tried to convince me they should arrange a match for me." She shivered at the concept.

"I thought that was only a mortal thing," I said, surprised. Political marriages were popular across men and gods alike. But human life was so short; should they marry wrong, it would not last forever. One or both would perish.

I remembered what Amun said about marriage. "Eternity is a long time to be married to the wrong person." He always encouraged gods to take their time.

It's partly why I had never given it much thought. My father had told me he was several decades old before he even considered settling down with a partner.

"Right?" Henet exclaimed. "But my mother, she really wants me to become some important deity. I think she regrets marrying a power level below her." There was bitterness in her tone. She was close with her father, and resented her mother's feelings about him. "Anyway…I'm not the right person to ask."

I found myself suddenly grateful that Shu's political dreams for me had never included marrying me off to "strengthen the court of Ra" or something. He married for love and wanted the same for his sisters.

"But I will say this, though," she said suddenly. "You could certainly do worse."

18

A CONFESSION

Once we landed, I decided to test out Hathor's hypothesis. Whether it was romantic or not, I was emotionally connected to Ptah. Theoretically, the all-seeing eye should be able to find him, blood relation or not. I focused on his essence, and his location appeared quicker than I expected. I knew him so well that when I saw the spot; I realized I should have been able to think of it on my own.

I found him at a waterfall at *Faiyum Oasis*. He often went there when he wanted to think. It was one of the first natural wonders he had ever made, and he said being near it made him remember the excitement of creation. It was easy as a god, doing the same thing for all of time, to become bored.

The oasis was also just a calming place, with the water brushing the stones below to emit a gentle bubbling sound. It was located in the center of a lake, where both the sun and moonlight would sparkle off the surface. It served as a reward, something special for people to find who made the journey.

I'm sure he heard me approach, but he said nothing.

"It's going to be harder to avoid me now," I joked.

"I don't think I've ever been too hard to find," he replied, not looking away from the water.

He wasn't wrong. Sekhmet had pointed it out, and now I realized just how often he had bent over backward to always be available for me, no matter the strange time or limited location options.

"I was…I was hoping to talk about the conversation the other night…" I felt a lump in my throat. I had never felt so awkward around him before. I couldn't figure out what to do with my hands; every posture felt strange.

"Yes?" He turned to look at me. I didn't see any anger in his eyes anymore, which was a good sign. They had regained their normal softness.

"I'm…I'm sorry for the way I spoke to you," I stammered. "It wasn't fair…you were just worried about me."

Everyone had been—Shu and Sekhmet's rescue had taught me that. But with him, it was different somehow.

He smiled, which I was grateful to see again. "I'm sorry too. Just the idea of you facing off against Apep…you and Sekhmet alone against him and his army—it terrified me. I…I don't know what I'd do without you, Bast."

"Yes, I am willing to admit that perhaps my actions were a bit immature. I just…unlocking this part of my magic made me feel more powerful, I guess?" I paused. "I have spent so much time stuck in limbo. Now that I have discovered the truth about everything, I want to unlock everything."

Ptah stepped a bit closer. "Well, if you remember, as immortals, we aren't exactly short on time."

"Perhaps I'm spending too much time around humans in Duat," I mused. "Everything for them is so fleeting. Some of the humans I see—their whole life is a blink for us. Why do we deserve more?"

He took a moment to answer. "Perhaps we don't deserve it. But it's what we have been given. All we can do is be responsible with that gift, I think."

"And responsibility does not equal running headlong into fights I can't win, you wager?" I asked, tone lighter again. I decided I would not tell him about my failed exhibition at Lake Nassor quite yet. I didn't want to see more disappointment on his face.

"Some might say that."

"I'm not going to stop looking for a way to stop him. I'm going to keep practicing with my powers, but...I'll be more careful," I promised, and I meant it.

"I am very relieved to hear that." We locked eyes. "And I apologize if, even for a moment, you felt I didn't believe in you. I just believe that even someone as phenomenal as you needs a bit of time to grow their gifts."

All of a sudden, my heart was beating faster. The tension had dissolved, so why was I so nervous? My sister's words kept echoing in my head. I stared into his eyes, but I knew that just looking into them would not lead to answers.

"Sekhmet mentioned something after you left…" I had thought of what I was going to say in Duat, but somehow I couldn't remember any of that now; my mind was blank. So just pushing forward, I realized, was the only way. "It's probably just her teasing me, very likely of course, but uh…she said you're…in love with me."

Ptah chuckled, but I did not see any surprise on his face. "It makes sense she'd catch on before you did."

It's true.

"Yes," he continued. "I have been in love with you for a very long time, Bastet."

Were the stars glowing brighter? It seemed like his eyes were sparkling all of a sudden. I felt an intensity in his look, but it did not scare me.

I became aware of how close we were standing. My heart was fluttering. For some reason, I wanted to be closer.

I realized I was supposed to say something back, but I had no idea what I was feeling, let alone words to contextualize it. I opened my mouth and then closed it again.

Ptah reached out his hand, as if to touch my face, and then stopped, holding it in the air. "You don't need to say anything right now," he whispered. "In fact, I don't want you to."

My mind jumped to the fact that I had seen his face when I was on the brink of death only one night ago. Should I mention that? It felt relevant. "Are you su—?" I started to say.

He cut me off. "I mean it. We've confirmed you can find me when you need. Come and seek me out, but when you're ready." He gave me one last long look.

And then he walked away, leaving me with nothing but my thoughts for company.

19

SEEKING ADVICE

The fluttering in my stomach was back. I thought I would feel a sense of closure at hearing the answer. But although I had heard his truth now, what was my own? Why hadn't I answered? What if he was hurt?

One way or another, it felt like everything was about to change. I paced around for a few minutes before deciding I couldn't just go back to my room yet.

With a few hours remaining until dawn, I found myself wandering somewhere where I could seek advice.

Shu's temple did not architecturally match ours, as it was commissioned when he married Tefnut, and therefore represented them both. Instead of a focus on letting in sunlight or rain, it was designed around letting in the breeze. One could open every window, no matter how huge. It was also the tallest in all of Egypt, so Shu could be close to the clouds.

Truth be told, I did not visit as much as a sister-in-law should. It wasn't intentional, but with my time so limited, I rarely wandered this far across the city. But he would not turn me away.

I entered through the living quarters' door and was quickly met by Tefnut.

She smiled upon seeing me. "Bastet, this is a lovely surprise!"

She was a cat deity like me and my sister. In fact, our father had made us somewhat resemble her when asked to picture our appearance by Amun, since there were few feline deities yet.

This had led to a few jokes upon their marriage that Shu was "basically marrying his sister", but he most certainly was not.

"My apologies for showing up without any notice…"

"Do not concern yourself; come on in," she gestured inside, and I followed.

My nephew Geb immediately tackled me in a hug once I crossed the threshold. "AUNT BAST!" he yelled.

I laughed. "Hi, Geb." He was a spitting image of Shu, except that on top of his head were the feathers of a goose instead of a peacock.

"How's Duat? Do you see dead people? Have you seen a snake?" He was full of energy, jumping up and down and rolling back and forth on his heels. He had a stuffed bird in his hands, which he kept shaking.

Tefnut softly instructed Geb to go to his room. "It's time for the adults to talk, alright?"

He pouted but ran off.

If I made it out of all this, I promised myself I would spend more time with him. He deserved a present aunt.

"Sorry about that," she said. "He's young, and can get a bit excited. Did Shu tell you he's started showing some signs of his power?"

"No, but that's great," I replied. "What is it?"

"Tides!" she said proudly. "Makes sense, really, when you put air and moisture together. I think he will be quite powerful. And also popular, which your brother might appreciate a bit more."

"That sounds about right." He had always told me that knowing the right person will always get you farther than knowing the right spell. I had never had enough time to prove or disprove the theory.

"Here, let me call him in here." She leaned down the hallway. "SHU! Your sister is here!"

Shu floated in, smiling when he saw me. "Look who it is."

Portraits covered the walls. Unlike my father's temple, they looked like they could be in an average mortal's home. There were no battle scenes or dramatic retellings. Some featured his wife and child, but I was also touched to see one of our family when it was whole. I rarely got to see my mother's face anymore.

I paused and looked at it for a moment long after Shu and Tefnut started walking into the dining room, before following them.

Tefnut was a great host, immediately pulling out a plate full of shortbread stuffed with sweet fruits and honey from another room. She even offered me some wine, explaining the servants had already left for the night. Not every god could afford a large staff.

"If this is business of the court of Ra, I can leave you be," she offered, standing by the entryway once she had laid out the table, and my brother and I were sitting on the antique plush chairs. The room was smaller and cozier than what I was used to.

I shook my head. "No, actually, I could use your input too."

She sat down next to Shu, who was watching me. "Not that I'm not happy to see you, but I assume you came over for more than our delicious honey cakes."

I wiped my mouth with a handkerchief. "Yes, well… Last night, Sekhmet brought something to my attention, and tonight Ptah confirmed it…"

"That he's in love with you?" Shu interjected, winking.

"Was everyone aware but me?" I asked, having to stop my mouth from falling open while I was eating. How blind was I, exactly?

Tefnut laughed, glancing over at him. "I assumed the same, to be fair."

"I was not sure you did," Shu clarified. "But it didn't feel like my place to tell you. I suppose someone had to if Ptah wasn't going to himself."

"I see…" My face felt warm.

Why didn't he tell me? On the one hand, I felt a little silly. It felt like another thing people had been hiding from me. But I am not sure that, before the argument, I would have believed anyone anyway.

"Well, you've got me more than curious now —how do you feel for him? What did you say?" Tefnut softly clapped her hands together in excitement.

"I didn't say…anything, actually. He told me not to respond right away. He said to think about it…" My heart sped up again at the recollection.

"And now you're spiraling," Shu guessed.

"That's a bit strong of a term," I contended, although he was right. "But I cannot seem to untangle my thoughts, that is correct." I pointed to the two of them. "When did you realize you were in love with each other?" I watched their reaction intently.

Shu laughed. "You are aware it doesn't usually happen at the same moment, yes? I could answer when it happened for me, but I will also let my wife answer for herself," he said, nodding in her direction.

Of course it doesn't... My face warmed again as I wished I had asked my question differently.

He turned to Tefnut and smiled. "For me, it was the first time I saw her interact with her followers at the Feast of the Nile. We were both around your age, if I remember right."

"Some gods, they only respond to the most extravagant sacrifices or requests. You of course, see this at the Solstice."

I nodded; this was especially true of the ancient gods. It seemed that over the decades, the gifts they received became commonplace, and they forgot the efforts humans made to procure them.

"And yet this goddess of mine took time to individually send down a sign of response to every single gift she received," he continued, his eyes seeming to brighten at the memory. "I think they told you that you couldn't do that again, do I have that right?"

She chuckled. "Yes, my mother told me that it was a 'waste of everyone's time' for me to send down a thanks for every single offering. But I was so excited, it was my first time as an of-age deity. I wanted the people to see how much I appreciated them trusting me with their gifts!"

She pointed to a wine bottle on a shelf near the window. "That's one of the first gifts I ever got. I've never wanted to drink it; it's better as a reminder."

"I still have never met someone who has such an appreciation for everything good in this world. I was drawn to that positivity, to that way of looking at the world." He turned to me. "Our father is very important. He has a stressful position among the gods, and I never wanted that. I never wanted to marry for power or something. I married to be happy."

I studied the way Tefnut watched him, a hint of that happiness evident just in her eyes as she listened to him speak. She reached out her hand on the table in his direction, and he took it.

It reminded me of the time Ptah had reached out his hand to me in the library.

"What about you?" I asked her.

"I think it took me a bit longer," she admitted. "But I will ask you the same thing my mother asked me. If Ptah came to you tomorrow and told you he had chosen a spouse, how would you feel?"

I tried to picture it. Ptah had no parents to pressure him into choosing a match. If other goddesses had caught his eye over the years, he had certainly never mentioned it. And I had only been around him with others at festivals.

"I…I don't know," I answered.

"Well, that's alright, Bastet. You are quite young," Tefnut said. "There is still a lot to learn."

It was the same thing Ptah had said—and they were both right, of course. Every night, I watched mortals leave the world at an age that was a blink of an eye to an immortal. But ever since I found out about Apep, I had felt like I was living in limbo. I was tired of waiting for answers.

That dawn, when I closed my eyes, I saw a grand wedding feast. At the end of the table, Ptah sat adorned in fine robes. I couldn't see who was beside him. Every time I tried, a fog appeared that wouldn't disappear until I looked away. If I tried to look down, I also could not see where I sat at the table. I kept trying, growing more frustrated each time, until I eventually woke up.

20

QUESTION OF THE HEART

The next night, my feet carried me back to my temple.

Usually, I came here to think of the future, to dream about who I would be once we were freed from Apep. But today, it brought me back to the past, when I first met Ptah...The first thing I remembered about that day was that he had shaken my hand.

"That's a bit formal," I giggled. Children rarely did such things.

"We are doing business," he had said, voice serious. "I want to tell you that I value the opportunity to do this work."

Although it was unusual, I appreciated the sentiment. It showed me the earnestness with which he approached life. I wasn't sure what to expect, meeting a god who had created himself.

It was that fact that gave us a quick connection. "Do you really not remember how you came to be?" I had asked once the initial pleasantries of our conversation were over. As a child, you are not held back by social conventions —I never would have been so blunt now.

"No, I do not," he had answered, still quite formal. "I'm aware it is strange. They say there is a part of Amun inside me that wants to focus on creation. But if such a thing were true, I have no memory of it. I have no idea when—or if—I will have the answers on it."

"I may not recall my creation, but it was strange too," I replied. I told him about how my sister and I only existed because Amun had answered my father's request. Even though we were born of ancient gods, my existence was an oddity. Sekhmet and I represented halves of our father, brought forth not by nature but by necessity. And now we lived in the space between god and half-god, growing up in a classification never before seen.

"Well, I think it's alright to be a little different," he had said once I was done. "I'd rather be strange than boring, wouldn't you?"

That was the moment I knew we would be friends. If you had told me that one day we might become more than that, would I have believed it?

When I stepped into the temple, several cats padded over to me and purred. Despite not seeing me often, they seemed to appreciate I had given them their home. Perhaps they could tell more than that. Perhaps they sensed my essence in them, our connection.

Pawarem jumped. "Goddess, I did not expect to see you tonight, pardon me!"

"Oh, don't worry, this isn't an official visit or anything," I said with a smile. "Though I was in fact hoping you would be here."

He bowed. "I am at your service."

"This may sound odd," I continued. "But I wanted to ask you something. This temple is a lot to manage for a single mortal. Oh, I didn't mean to imply you couldn't or—"

Pawarem laughed. "I am not offended, goddess."

"Right, well, anyway, what I meant was, does Ptah come here? Independent of me, I mean." I tried to keep my tone casual.

He tilted his head. "Well, of course, do you not notice the new enclosures for the cats each time you come? How they change in size, and are they always clean and well-maintained? He comes frequently to check on the cats and uses his abilities to make them comfortable."

My eyes widened as I looked around, as though seeing the room for the first time. How had I never noticed? Each cat had its own little den, lined with linen bedding, with food and water bowls neatly placed. Shelves traced the walls, giving them space to leap and play.

"There is more goddess, if you wish for me to tell you," he continued.

"More?" I tore my eyes away from the cats.

"Yes, well, it's meant to be a surprise until the day you ascend, but... Given the way you have come to me tonight..." He hesitated, then nodded, as though convincing himself. "I think you need to see it now." He gestured for me to follow him into the archive room.

I couldn't help but notice the stack of new prayer requests sitting on the stone table, but forced myself to ignore them. Pawarem opened a drawer in one of the cases and pulled out a different, neatly organized pile of papyrus. He made space on the table, pushing aside some ink, and placed it down.

"What is this?" I asked, walking closer to the table.

"This, goddess Bastet, is what Ptah calls the 'Persea' prayer requests from your people." Seeing my face was still blank with confusion, he continued, "As I am sure you've heard, the Persea tree blooms regardless of the season. It lives throughout the colds of winter and the heat of summer."

I nodded; I was familiar with it. Pharaohs viewed it as a symbol of vitality and divine connection to the gods, due to its ability to endure forever.

"These requests are like that," he explained. "They are not timely, more like wishes. The thought is that once you come into your full powers, you could answer these right away. So, your people can understand you have been listening to them all along."

I carefully picked up the first parchment and opened it. It had the messy handwriting of a child. The message was: "Dear Goddess Bastet, can you please bless our cat sanctuary in the middle of the city, so that more mice spawn in the area, and it is protected from the elements? Thank you."

I clutched the request to my chest, a mix of emotions washing over me. Part of me wished I could have answered this prayer myself.

But the fact that Ptah had stepped in and done this made my heart feel lighter.

"Goddess, I do hope we have not overstepped." The priest seemed cautious. "I've been helping Ptah in this mission…"

"You have not overstepped," I assured him, beaming. "This is…amazing. I just had no idea." I glanced at the stack again. He had done so many of them.

"I truly believe he wants to see your happiness."

And yet I never saw it.

I smiled. "That's what I'm learning."

After spending some time with the cats, I returned to my father's temple and went to my bedroom. Sleep still felt far away. My mind was more worked up than ever after the visit to my temple.

I pulled out my painting supplies.

I began sketching the scene from my dream—the grand table and high vaulted ceilings. If my dreams were trying to send me a message, as they were supposed to do, they were not doing so successfully. Perhaps painting them would bring it into focus, completing the puzzle pieces my visit to Shu and conversation with Khonsu had provided.

My arms were still sore from climbing the tree at the lake. Despite that, the brush still glided smoothly, and for a while, I found myself getting lost in the colors and strokes.

It was certainly one of my better paintings. Normally, I stuck to landscapes or still life, leaving the emotional ventures to Ptah. I usually struggle with faces. But these were etched into my memory.

Around the table, I painted the faces I had seen at the festival. The answer grew obvious as I reached the end; there was a reason Sekhmet and Shu were in attendance. My heart pounded as I recreated Ptah in his grand robes. For now, the only empty seat was the one next to him.

I closed my eyes again and immersed myself in the mental image. Finally seeing the full picture, I smiled, opened my eyes, and slowly painted myself sitting next to him.

The image felt whole, and for a moment so did I.

My first instinct told me to put down the paintbrush and run across Heliopolis to find him.

But my feet stayed rooted in place. What kind of partner could I be? I didn't have access to a full life. I was living within the confines of a curse. Would choosing him mean condemning him to share my doom, always wanting more?

How could I do that to my best friend? Ask him to live much of his life without his partner by his side?

Discovering this truth didn't change the fact that I couldn't offer him all of me.

Two days later, Duat swelled with more mortal souls than normal. Father had warned me of this the night before. There had been a human scuffle between warring territories. Nothing major, no gods were involved on either side.

While a resolution had been found, it was not after the loss of several dozen soldiers. Many of them were young, of course, but the things they had seen gave them the appearance of someone older.

I did not enjoy nights like these, where death was everywhere. But it was a relief to have something to throw myself into that wasn't my thoughts about Ptah or the ever-looming threat.

One of the younger men who had lost his life in the battle rode close to us, gripping the sides of the boat in fear. His face was scarred but smooth, without a single wrinkle of age.

I gave him the usual greeting, but he did not seem to hear it or process exactly what was happening. "Please, you have to send me back," he pleaded. "I haven't had enough time."

"That is not in my power," I said apologetically. "The gods may gift you with reincarnation, should you be found worthy." I regretted the words the moment they left my mouth, with reincarnation being such a rare gift given to mortals.

"I just reunited with my family," he explained to me, his voice breaking. "We had a falling out. I wasted so many days away from them over troubles that did not matter. I finally saw the way before the attack. I told them I would come over for dinner once the fighting was over. They begged me to come sooner, but I was convinced there was so much…time left…and…" He put his head in his hands.

My heart ached for him, but not wanting to make any more false promises, I just said, "You may all be reunited eventually in paradise."

He lifted his head. "Then my waiting will be penance," he said, slowly beginning to drift away. I was convinced there was so much time left.

Why was I acting like I had all the time in the world? I was immortal, yes—but one with a deadline sprawled before me. If I didn't defeat Apep, I too would be leaving this world, bound to judgment, at an age young for even mortals.

What was I waiting for?

Henet walked up to me and gently placed her hand on my shoulder. "Bastet, are you alright? You're shaking…"

"I may not have forever," I mumbled.

"What are you—?"

I turned to her. "I'm not wasting time."

The second we touched land, I used the all-seeing eye to locate Ptah. And then I ran.

My feet barely touched the ground as I followed the light taking me in his direction. I kept seeing the regret in the mortal's eyes. I would not let that become my fate.

I burst into the dining room, startling Ptah so much that he nearly dropped the goblet in his hand. I couldn't remember ever running this fast or being this out of breath. "Bastet, is everything alright?" he asked.

"I…love…you…too!" I gasped, having to stop and catch my breath between each word.

Ptah stood up and caught me in his arms. He tilted my face up. "I'd kiss you, but you seem to be struggling to breathe already."

I blushed and then laughed. "I can do that later."

He leaned in and pressed his lips to mine. I hadn't spent much time imagining what kissing would feel like. But the best way to describe it was the electrifying touch of the sun on my skin, the rare times I got to experience it. It was both natural and novel at the same time.

After a few moments, he pulled away. We sat down together on a lounge chair in the corner. It was as though we both instinctively knew we wanted to sit close, not separated by the inches the chairs would hinder us.

"What made you realize?" Ptah asked.

I told him about the dreams, the painting, and the man in Duat. "What about you? When did you realize?"

He smiled. "Do you remember that day you asked me to add a cat sanctuary to your temple?"

"Of course." Even at a young age, I knew that domestic cats would someday fall under my domain. I saw no reason to delay taking care of them, especially since it was something that could be managed without my presence or even the use of magic.

He placed his hand over mine. "The way you cared so much for small creatures, treating them as we do our followers, I saw your heart that day forward. But we were young then—I thought it was just a crush."

"But it didn't go away?"

"No, it most certainly did not. However, when you didn't seem to return my feelings, I tried to move on. I even considered reaching out to a matchmaker…"

There was no doubt now about what Tefnut asked me. The idea of someone else being with Ptah put my stomach in knots. "Why didn't you just tell me earlier?"

"Truth be told, I never wanted to ruin our friendship. I would think of times, feel moments, but then they would slip through my fingers. I told myself that maybe once you ascended, it would make more sense. We'd have more time to figure things out naturally."

This was fair; I had worried about the same thing. "Are you sure you want me as only half a god?" I asked nervously.

"Bastet, all I mean is that I want every moment with you I can have. If those moments are fleeting, I do not care. I will cherish all that you are willing to give." He squeezed my hand.

"I will give you all I can," I promised, though my voice was strained. I couldn't give him as much as I wanted, not until the curse was broken.

21

AN ULTIMATUM

As dawn approached, I ran across the city to Thoth's temple. The last thing I wanted to do was pass out somewhere on the street, but I had to risk it. I had no desire to get on Thoth's bad side and it was time to return the prophecy. I could see the sun at the bottom of the horizon as I arrived, breathless, in the front entryway.

Luckily, one of Thoth's priests was on his way inside and offered to take the prophecy scroll for me the rest of the way. I didn't recognize him, but Thoth's court was huge. With so little time left, I handed it over to him, offered a quick thank you, and began running back to Ra's temple.

I felt lighter without it in my possession, a physical representation that I didn't need to have it anymore. As the sky shifted from darkness to the orange of sunrise, I fell asleep at the doorway of my bedroom.

This emotion followed me during my time in Duat. I felt a sense of calm I hadn't had since the day I stormed into my father's office. The anger was gone. Members of the crew commented on my smile. When we reached land, I planned to tell Father he didn't need to worry anymore—the fight wasn't over, a deadline still loomed, but I would take advantage of the time we had left and do it right.

That night, I was standing by the edge of the boat, humming. My mind flew away into a daydream about my upcoming evening with Ptah. He was going to cook for us. Most gods left that to servants, but Ptah viewed food as another instrument to create art.

I was trained in vigilance, but my mind was lost to the negligence of my heart.

I was raised better.

And so I missed it.

I blinked as the smell of death suddenly filled my nostrils. My veins turned cold as I saw glowing red eyes. A demon boat was next to the Meseket. The vessel was not large and imposing, but small and sleek, with room for perhaps a handful of crew members, and camouflage in the night.

How could I have been so reckless?

I blinked again, and a demon was trying to board, a converted human with terrifying speed. A demon is a soul judged and determined to be evil. Normally, Anubis ensured their souls were devoured so they ceased to exist, denied a peaceful afterlife.

But sometimes Apep got a hold of them first, meaning their eyes glowed bright red, as the only thing fueling them was his power. There was no more life moving them, though no one knew for certain whether the mortal's consciousness remained buried deep inside.

The demon was an older man, dressed in armor with Apep's symbol engraved on it. I was quicker than him and blocked him from boarding by planting myself on the edge and holding my spear firmly, facing his direction, mere inches from his face.

"Bastet, do not push him!" Father yelled, and so I did not lunge with my spear. I held my ground, daring the demon to move. If he took another step, I did not care for my own safety, but it seemed like he seemed to hold.

The demon opened his mouth, but the voice that came out was clearly not his. It was the booming, deep voice of the god of chaos. "Ra and his foolish child, you have made a grave error. Did you think you could forever hide the words of your prophecy? Was I content with the limbo Amun has trapped us in? It is time for you to face me, and to end this."

My father bristled. I had never seen him look away from the sun during our journey, but he made direct eye contact with the demon. "You do not give orders here, Apep."

The creature made a sound that could be called a laugh, though it was also like he was gasping for air. Apep's voice then resumed. "I suspected you would not see the reason, so I have decided to add some motivation. That is why I took the opportunity this evening to invite Shu over for a visit. Well, by 'invited,' I mean my demons snatched him. You have ten days before harm comes to him."

The sun was going to fall. I saw my father's hands shake, and the ball of light began to slip. I was terrified to move, in case the demon would attempt to board if I was not facing the tip of my spear. But if the sun fell into the waves, we would have to stop the boat. Until we retrieved it from the dark waters, it would not rise, and the mortals would wake up to darkness.

I did something I had never done before. I released the spear. I did not watch it land but trusted it hit the demon's heart as I heard him fall in the water off the boat. I used all my speed and dexterity to leap, kneel, and somehow catch the sun mere seconds before it would hit the waves.

It was heavier than I had expected. The heat was powerful but did not burn. Looking at it, however, was painful for my eyes, and because of its size, it was all I could see, filling my vision. I was grateful when my father carefully took it back and returned it to its proper position.

"Thank you, daughter. You have honored the people of Egypt."

He paused, and I felt a brief swell of pride. But now was not the time.

He spoke in a calming voice. "I need to ask you to do something difficult with me now. Do you understand? Despite what we have just heard, we must finish this journey. We must do our duty and set the sun in its proper place before we react to what we have just heard."

I nodded, though he was right in that he had never asked me to do anything more difficult. I wanted nothing more than to chase after the demon boat that had rowed away. To corner the crew and force them to take me to my brother, to tear apart Apep's lair until I was sure Shu had not been harmed.

Instead, I paced up and down the length of the boat, looking at no one, speaking to no one.

But we finished the ride.

The mortals would likely not notice the minutes-long delay that greeted them at dawn. The only ones who might be the scribes of astronomy, who might jot it down as a strange anomaly, and show no further interest. Their history books would not include that this was the day the gods were thrust into crisis.

Using one of Thoth's messenger birds—which my father could access on demand—we sent a message to Sekhmet and found her in my father's war room when we returned. She had her head in her hands and jumped up when we entered.

I had barely sat down before he asked me, "Bastet, are you able to locate him with your all-seeing eye?"

"My…what?" My eyes widened. While that, of course, had been my first plan the moment we landed, I had never told him of my power. I looked at Sekhmet, who shrugged.

Had Hathor betrayed my confidence? I had come to her under false pretenses, but the thought still stung.

"Heka informed me. Obviously, I was going to keep tabs on your efforts. Do not worry about that now—answer my question." He crossed his arms.

That answer was less surprising. Heka had not exactly given me the sense of someone harboring a trustworthy ear.

"When did you find out?" I asked, shoulders slumping.

My father shook his head. "Look for your brother, Bastet." His tone held finality.

I closed my other eye and focused my thoughts on Shu—on my brother's face, the wind that carried him, the essence of his spirit. The image was slow, like fog clearing, and then I saw what appeared to be an underground metal cell. Inside, Shu was meditating. It was no surprise he was calmer than most would be in such a place.

I forced the image to expand more, even as my head began to ache with effort. I had to ensure he was actually alright.

"He's uninjured," I said, relieved. The heaviness in my chest lessened slightly. At least he was alive. There was time. I described to them what I saw.

"Can you see where this cell is?" my father asked.

I opened my eyes again, and my vision was slightly blurry. "So far, I have only been able to conjure images that resemble a painting; it shows the person and what's around them, but that's it. However, I have noticed that as I go to the places in my head, I see a light that guides me."

"So, we will at least be able to tell whether we are headed in the right direction," Sekhmet mused.

"It's a start," my father agreed. But his voice sounded deflated.

Had he been hoping for more? Or is he just worried?

"I will keep practicing," I promised. "I may be able to get a wider angle; this is all still very… new."

I had no idea how clear or close an image I could procure, but I had to try.

"Good, we will need every advantage we can get."

"Did I see in your message that the prophecy leaked somehow? How did that even happen?" Sekhmet asked, turning to me.

I thought back to who had actually seen the prophecy besides me. Not that I had any reason to distrust him, but Ptah had visited me when I was reviewing records, though I never read him the full details. He hadn't even seen the parchment. I had only had the thing for a handful of days myself. Suddenly, realization hit me like a chilly wind.

"The priest…"

"What?"

"I…when I went to return the prophecy, I didn't go all the way into Thoth's temple. There was this, this man outside, and he said he would turn it in for me. I was in a hurry, it was almost dawn; he looked like he worked for Thoth's court…" My chest tightened.

Replaying the moment in my head, there had been something dark about the man's eyes. Why hadn't I waited another day? Surely Thoth would have understood, given my limitations.

Sekhmet flared her nostrils and opened her mouth to speak, but my father held up his hand to silence her. "We do not need to focus on what we cannot change. We must move forward."

She clenched her jaw and looked away. I was grateful for his intervention; she would not have listened to anyone else. I could only hope that whatever she was holding in would be directed toward the wayward priest, or even better, our future enemies, and not me.

Why isn't he the one yelling at me?

Maybe he saw the fear in my eyes, the shame weighing down my whole body. The idea of Shu being behind bars, in the den of demons and an evil god, was inconceivable.

He continued, "You must prepare yourselves to go to battle. Sekhmet, you will train your sister in combat. Bastet, I want you to recruit anyone you can to join you. The major gods are less likely to want to get involved, but some feel loyalty to me. More will be interested in saving Shu. Minor gods are always seeking to prove themselves; you likely will have better luck there."

I was finally getting the training I asked for in this very chair when I confronted my father about the prophecy. But there was no sense of victory in getting what I wanted. No relief at being taken seriously.

Because now I understood what we were facing. Now I knew how little power and knowledge I truly had.

None of that mattered, though. I would fight for my brother.

I was unsure why he asked me to handle recruitment; I had far less contact with the gods compared to him and Sekhmet. He was right; Shu was very popular, which would help. He never said no to helping others out on their own missions. He didn't do it to garner goodwill, but he had certainly done it.

But we needed as much help as we could get.

Sekhmet voiced what I had planned to leave unspoken. "Father, how much will you be able to fight with us? Without the sun?"

He furrowed his brow. "Not as much as I would like, daughter. But I will do whatever it takes to see my son return home."

It was clear the conversation was ending, as our father stared out the window, lost in thought. Sekhmet stood up first. When she was at the door to the war room, she turned around and looked at me. "Training starts the moment you land tomorrow," she stated, shoulders tight, and eyes narrowed.

Following her out, my head spun at everything we had discussed. Ten days to form some kind of divine fighting force, as well as learn how to land a finishing blow on the god of chaos, so I could save my brother.

I was halfway out the door when I remembered Ptah was waiting for me for our date.

22

A FIRST ATTEMPT

Cursing under my breath, I sprinted across the temple, begging my legs to move faster.

Why didn't I send a messenger bird? I had literally watched my father send one to Sekhmet before. What was I thinking? Will he even still be there?

I had planned to dress up for my first date. I even had a nice hairpiece picked out. I wanted everything to be perfect.

Instead, my brother got kidnapped. So not only was I in my normal, drab leather armor and tunic, but I hadn't even had a moment to look in a mirror. My knee also scraped from when I landed on the deck after catching the sun.

This night was not going how I imagined it.

Finally reaching the door, I thrust it open so quickly that I nearly slipped.

Inside, the table was all set up, complete with candles and some of the nice porcelain plates I hadn't seen in ages. Goblets sat next to my favorite bottle of wine.

On top of that, it smelled phenomenal. I didn't recognize the type of fish at first, but it was as if all the sweet smells of the sea had traveled with it. It was accompanied by vegetables and the freshest looking bread I had ever seen.

My eyes finally found him, sitting near the end of the table.

He's still here!

"Oh, Ptah, it looks wonderful," I said, taking a deep breath. The food had likely cooled by now, which I felt guilty about. How long has he been waiting?

He looked a little dejected, his eyes clouded. He sat up as he saw me, but didn't immediately stand. "I thought…I thought maybe you weren't going to come. That maybe you'd changed your mind about this, about us…"

"Oh no, oh no, I am so sorry." I walked over to him, wanting him to see the truth in my eyes. "I should have sent word. There is a crisis in the house of Ra. Things have been moving so fast, I didn't…I wasn't paying attention to the time and—"

His face shifted to concern. "What happened?"

I told him everything, starting with the demon boat, the sun slipping, and our family's discussion after we came back from Duat. Saying it all out loud made the emotions hit me again, and I quickly checked on Shu's location with the all-seeing eye; luckily, there was no change. He is still alive.

I had a feeling I would be reassuring myself a lot with that sight over the upcoming days.

Ptah didn't say anything at first. Instead, he closed the gap between us and wrapped his arms around me.

For the first time in hours, I felt like I could breathe. I closed my eyes and tried to clear my mind. I hadn't realized my eyes had started to water until I wiped the tears away. I wanted to be present at this moment. Ptah had always been there for me. He had seen me cry, and he had listened to me.

But now that we were evolving the nature of our relationship, there was something more intimate in this moment. No one else could make me feel so safe, no one else saw all of me the way he did.

"Apologies for dampening our spirits a bit," I said after a pause. "Not quite the typical first date for the girl to burst in late, talking about ultimatums from evil chaos gods."

"A typical first date sounds dreadfully boring," he responded with a small smile. "We are years past small talk, anyway." He winked.

That was true.

His voice turned serious again. "I just wish I could be a part of this team you're forming. I want to protect you. But…"

But he had no combat skills. Not only were none of his powers useful in a fight, but he also had no training beyond the basics for self-defense. Even less than I had received when I was young.

Truthfully, it was one of my favorite things about him. He never spoke about war or obsessed over physical strength. He was still incredibly masculine, but in a way that felt different from other young male gods.

"Ptah, it's alright. You don't have to protect me. Your emotional support is more than enough. I can't exactly cry like this in front of Sekhmet at training tomorrow."

I could see it already, her rolling her eyes and telling me to get over myself. It's not that she was cruel. She had also supported me plenty over the years. But it was different. Her love came in actions such as staying late to help me with schoolwork or bringing me a book I'd been looking for. Comfort and Empathy? Not her forte.

He laughed. "I suppose she wouldn't be as comforting," he agreed. "But I will find a way to help you, Bastet. I swear it."

I believed him. "Let us try our first date again after I've saved my brother and killed a god?" I offered.

He smiled. "I look forward to that."

I wish it were that simple—that all I had to do is run an errand, and we could try again. I didn't let myself dwell on the thought that this might have been our only chance at a date at all. That if we failed to take down Apep, there would be no redo.

Instead, I exclaimed, "Now let's eat!"

23

TRAINING

I showed up to the first night of training with my spear and some old armor that barely fit, not sure what to expect. The training grounds for Ra's armies stretched across a giant field between his temple and Sekhmet's.

Sections were roped off for practicing certain skills—targets for practicing archery, stones of various sizes to work on strength, and cloth dummies strung up on sticks for stabbing drills.

It was clearly utilized most often during the day. Torches lined the field, some glowing with Ra's special flames, which shone brighter than ordinary fire.

About thirty of Sekhmet's soldiers were sparring when I arrived. They briefly stopped to bow their heads before snapping back to their practice. Many wielded swords, but a few half-gods used magic. I watched in awe as a woman with the head of a polar bear shot out flying icicles at her opponent, who dodged with expert precision.

I appreciated that they were on my side, but my stomach still twisted in knots. I felt like a kid playing dress-up.

My sister walked up to me and immediately pointed at my spear. "You're still using that thing?"

I rolled my eyes. "What is wrong with it? It helped me defend against the demon yesterday." I demonstrated with a quick stab at the air, trying to hide that I was nervous.

"Yes, it worked as a defense tool. But look at how dull that tip is? It surprises me even you managed to land it inside him, which I guess is impressive in itself." She walked to a nearby chest and pulled out a lance.

"Let's use this today," she instructed. "I'm not sure what the right fit will be, but we don't have a lot of time to find out."

I had never even used a lance. Why couldn't I just get a new spear? But pushing back this early in the night would only cause tension. So I just nodded. When this went wrong, I'd bring it up then.

"But we aren't going to practice killing blows today," she continued. "This may disappoint you…but you aren't ready for that yet."

I found it harder to bite my tongue. "We have ten days, sister. When am I going to be ready?"

"Bastet, ten days or not, if you tried to land a blow on anyone here, they'd have you on the ground before you could even blink. I don't care how much time wee have; we will start with the basics, just like with any other soldier."

"Basics? I learned the basics when I was ten. If I remember correctly, I picked up dodging a lot faster than you." It was true. From the very start of our education, we both lived up to our designated roles rather quickly.

"Alright, want to prove it?" Her face was too smug for my liking.

"Sure—if that's what it takes for you to teach me something actually useful," I snapped.

"Then let's see you use your cat instincts," Sekhmet said.

"What?" Truthfully, the only one I used regularly was my night vision.

"Oh, come on, 'cats thrive in the night' remember? One of the reasons is our stalking abilities. The ability to walk swiftly and quietly, moving with stealth, sometimes the element of surprise can make all the difference between victory and defeat."

She motioned toward the polar bear half-god, who was still focused on her practice.

Sekhmet lowered her voice. "That's Naliah. I want you to sneak up on her and trip her."

"What if I hurt her?" I whispered back. We had been taught that attacking from behind was poor fight etiquette.

She chuckled. "Somehow, I think she will be just fine, sister. Besides, do you think our enemies would be against such tactics? You said you didn't want the same training we had as children. Also, I'm not saying to stab her."

I dropped my spear. It was easier to stay light-footed with nothing in my hands. At first, I approached slowly, but then in the last few feet, I started to rush her, getting ready to kick out a foot and try to trip her.

But she was faster. Swinging around with a speed I wouldn't have anticipated from her size, she spun around and tackled me to the ground before I could blink.

"Ow…" I was suddenly very grateful I was decked out in armor.

Naliah's eyes widened as she recognized me. "Goddess Bastet, my deepest apologies, I had no idea it was you…" She offered a hand to help me up.

I took it and shook my head. "You have done nothing wrong; it was Sekhmet's idea." I glared at my sister, who was laughing. Attempting to maintain decorum, I shook some of the sand out of my armor.

I marched over to Sekhmet, nostrils flaring. "What was the point of that? Just to embarrass me?"

"I think you did that all on your own, sister," she replied, crossing her arms.

"That's not an answer. You set me up to fail." People were still watching us, but I didn't care. Their first impression of me was already ruined.

"No, I set you up to learn a lesson. I asked you if you wanted to prove yourself, you said yes, and then I allowed you to do just that." I could tell she was suppressing a smirk. I wanted to tackle her.

She was good at twisting things. But she could've had me fight against her, or with someone more privately located. "You're angry at me, aren't you?" I demanded, walking close to her.

"That's why you're doing this?"

"Why would I be angry at you, Bastet?" Sekhmet said with an exasperated huff. She then also noticed the small crowd watching us and gestured toward the outside of the field. "If we're going to do this, let's at least have the decency to do it in private, yes?"

I begrudgingly followed her. What I was about to say next shouldn't be said in front of an audience.

"Now I repeat, why would I be angry with you?" She crossed her arms.

"Because this is all my fault." I felt a lump in my throat. "Shu has been taken. I gave that fake priest, spy, whatever he is, the copy of the prophecy. If I hadn't done that…"

"Then our brother would be safe," Sekhmet finished. "To tell the truth, Bastet, I was fairly angry with you when I parted ways with you last night."

"So, you admit it!" But there was no triumph in the confirmation.

"Sure, if that's what you're looking for, yes, I admit it. I kept asking myself how you could be so irresponsible." Sekhmet kicked some sand in front of her. "But you know what I realized before I went to sleep?" She softened her tone a bit. "I can't say I would've done anything differently."

"Really?"

She sighed. "I also feel that rush to finish what I am doing before dawn. On top of that, Thoth is usually quite meticulous with whom he employs. I could sit here and tell you that, of course, I would pick up some kind of darkness in his eyes, but…I can't."

"I wish more than anything I could go back," I said quietly. "Make myself take a few more steps. If I passed out on the way back to our temple, who cares? At least Shu would be safe. Or, if I had just waited another day and explained to Thoth —" I stared off into the dark.

Sekhmet uncrossed her arms, saying, "Father was right, you can't stay fixated on the past. Continuing to run over scenarios that did not come to be will not bring our brother back."

I felt my eyes begin to water, so I looked away. "I can't figure out how to forgive myself."

"That is something you must accomplish yourself. But I promise you, my training exercises are not full of malice. I do not hold any true anger. We are on the same team. If you want to make it up to me, to Shu, to yourself? Let us prepare the best we can and then go and get him back."

It felt as if now was the moment to lay all things bare. "Can I ask you something else first?"

"If you'd like." She tilted her head.

"I understand that you were angry with me for a moment, which I deserve. But…have you ever been mad at Father?"

I worried the question would ruin whatever tenuous understanding had formed between us. But her answer was calm. "You mean about the prophecy?"

"Yes. I was wondering if…you never told me how that night went, when you filled in for me at Duat. I've had to learn a lot about maturity the last couple of weeks…But I have felt so alone in being angry at him. Is it so childish that I felt that way?"

"You're not alone," she promised me. "But I have always clung to my respect and duty over my feelings. Without you, we wouldn't have discovered the truth. That night, I planned to demand answers until I got one that made sense. But instead, I just listened to his empty platitudes and left feeling no better than when I boarded."

What? But Sekhmet isn't afraid of anyone.

She held out her hand to me. "Come on, let's go back."

I sniffed, grabbing it. "Was that polar bear at least your best fighter?" I asked, shifting back to our training. I hoped the answer would make me feel better.

She chuckled. "Naliah is extraordinary with her ice powers, but I would not say she is the best at hand-to-hand combat, no."

"Oh."

That's a bit embarrassing.

"Are we ready to review the basics now?" she asked, eyebrows raised.

I wiped the last bit of moisture from my eyes. "Bring on the basics."

24

A CALL TO WAR

The rest of the training went about as well as my failed stealth approach. I was still decent at dodging, but rusty. I would notice an attack a half-second too late, so I might miss a blow, but still be in a position for an easy follow-up.

I hated to admit it, but I was also starting to agree with Sekhmet that the spear was not the right weapon for me. Watching some of the more seasoned soldiers using them, I saw that it was useful for catching someone before they got too close or even throwing at a faraway opponent.

But for achieving what the prophecy dictated? I was meant to deliver the final blow, to end the fight. A faraway one-shot throw wasn't likely to end the god of chaos.

After three hours, I was exhausted.

Sekhmet noticed this, and I expected her to chastise me, as she had said the session would last four hours. But instead, she said, "Go get some rest, sister. We can stop here for today."

I hated that she was taking pity on me. We didn't have time for pity. But I also didn't have any energy left. "Tomorrow will go better," I promised.

"We can only hope."

"How is training going?" Ptah asked, waiting for me outside the grounds. His eyes lit up when he saw me.

I told him about my frustrations. "Turns out, spending every evening on a boat in the underworld does not automatically make you a competent fighter."

We walked over to a bench outside the temple and sat down. Ptah carried a small package.

"What if I'm not good enough?" I whispered, putting my head in my hands. "It's just my brother…I'm supposed to fulfill some ancient prophecy, and I got tackled on my first day of training."

"Bastet, you do not need to be the strongest fighter to win this battle," he insisted, putting his arm around me. "You only need to use your skills and land the finishing blow. That's all the prophecy dictates."

I leaned into him. "Yes, a feat I am not sure I can achieve…like you said, all I have is this magical eye and a shield that I can't make last for more than a few minutes…it's not enough!"

No, I will NOT tear up again.

"I was wrong to say that," Ptah replied. "Who am I to speak, when I have no combat or defense powers?"

"No, I needed to hear what you said. I don't have anything that can do actual damage…"

"Well, I might have something to help with that." He pulled out the cedar box and laid it in front of me on my lap.

"What?" My ears perked up.

I opened the box carefully. Inside, wrapped in thick fabric, there were two matching daggers. Their beauty immediately struck me. The silver was smooth, and the point was so sharp I did not want to test them. The pommels on them were fierce-looking domestic cats. The Eye of Ra was carved into the sides.

As I held onto the helm, it was clear these daggers were custom-made for me. They fit in my hand as if they had always been mine. As I moved my hands, it was fluid. They were lightweight, yet clearly powerful.

They were also beautiful.

"These are… Did you craft these?" I asked, although the answer seemed clear.

Ptah shrugged, watching me intently. "Yes."

"I've never seen you make a weapon before" I remarked, still in awe.

"Well, I figured it was time to learn," He responded. "Those blades are coated in a mix of ground-up materials that are toxic to snakes, like narcissus and philodendron. There's more of it in the bottle there. I figured it might give you a little bit of an edge, at least."

I had never heard of what I assumed was a plant, but I trusted he had done his research.

"Ptah, this is…this is amazing." I placed the daggers back into the box carefully and closed it before reaching out to embrace him. "Thank you."

He hugged me in return. "I had to be with you somehow, even though I can't fight. This was the only way I could think of how to do so."

"You will be with me in my thoughts," I promised. "Especially when I'm landing my excellent final stab with these."

He laughed. "Yes, please think of me when the blood of your enemies is hitting the ground."

I had asked the most powerful gods of Egypt to meet me in my father's banquet hall.

I initially resented this task. Not only did I have fewer connections than the rest of my family, but it felt like a waste of time. I had planned to use every moment I had to spare to train. Especially now that I had a new weapon, I lacked experience in wielding it. A part of me worried my father just asked me to do this so I would be "out of the way" while the real fighters practiced.

But then I remembered the voice of my popular political brother speaking to me. "Don't rule out the power of a good dinner, sister. A good meal with the right people at the table can win a war that hasn't even begun."

And so, I sat with Hathor at the head of the grand table, watching the servants lay out gold goblets and our finest bottles of wine. I needed someone who could throw a proper party, and she had agreed right away.

If she was angry about me leading her astray with the training, she did not mention it. "I think we're going to have a good crowd tonight," she assured me, as gods started to file in to the room.

"Whatever you wrote in that ibis message seems to have worked."

I recognized several faces right away. Montu was here; Sekhmet had kept her word on that one. I also saw some other war and combat gods, such as the powerful Horus and Anuket, the protector of the southern Egyptian border.

But I did not recognize them all, a fact that encouraged me. I had told people to invite anyone they wanted to hear out the call to arms from the house of Ra.

This was not like the time I had spoken to Ra's priests and advisors. No one stopped talking when I entered. Many of them outranked me, and even though I was the sun god's daughter, until I received my full powers, I was little more than a half-deity in their eyes.

But they showed up, I reminded myself. That had to count for something.

I positioned myself at the front end of the table and lifted a wine glass and a fork. After taking a deep breath, I clinked the fork against the glass. This caught the attention of those sitting near the front, eventually causing everyone to look.

"Thank you for being here today. While I am not my father, I do represent the house of Ra as I speak to you today about our mission. Many of you are aware of the…curse placed on my sister and me. For the course of our lives, there has been a stalemate between Apep and our house. That stalemate is set to come to an end."

Everyone was listening, which I appreciated, but I couldn't tell their reaction to my words. I cleared my throat. "A couple of days ago, a demon of Apep approached my father and me in Duat. He informed us that he captured Shu and promised he would come to no harm if I agreed to face him within ten days."

"Why does he wish to face you in particular?" Horus asked.

I told everyone about the prophecy, careful not to reveal how I had found out about it. "As you can see," I concluded, "I must land the finishing blow. If he…eliminates me, there is no more risk to him. He will likely use the opportunity to make a move on my father."

"I do not mean offense," Anuket spoke up. "But why would we want to involve ourselves in this conflict?" Anuket was famous for both his defensive powers and his army. "To join you would put our own lives at risk. Should the worst come to pass, and Ra were to fall, he would come for all of us next."

There were some murmurings of agreement among the other guests.

I had expected this question. Gods were not all that different from mortals when it came to altruism—they cared for their family, and valued alliances, but they often needed additional motivation to take action for those outside of those groups.

"There are two answers I can offer to that," I responded. You have to get this part right.

"One, should Ra fail, there is no promise he won't come for you, whether you have joined us or not." I relayed the part of the prophecy where it confirmed the sky would turn red and then fall into darkness, the very image that haunted my nightmares. Would it scare them too?

"With all of the world turned to night, he will have immense power—and is likely to wield it farther than just the destruction of the light." I did not want to spark fear, but I also knew I needed to impart on them the right amount of danger.

I was asking them to risk their lives. I could not stand up here and hide that.

"There is a good chance he will stop with my family when he comes to take his revenge."

I let the words sit and felt their eyes on me. They were at least listening. But I did not see any nods or smiles.

Time to try another approach.

"But if the worst case is not something that motivates you, I ask you to think of…victory. The reverse is also true upon Apep's defeat. My father's harnessing of light will only grow stronger. He would be happy to share some of that magic with those who stand with us. You will be able to add light powers to your already strong arsenals to fight your own enemies and protect your own people."

It was not a concept I had run past my father, but I knew he would understand that I had to say all I could.

I was not sure which reason landed stronger with the guests, but when I finally sat back down, a line formed in front of me. But it did not matter why.

The gods of Egypt were showing up for us.

25

A LOOK AT THE STARS

Still riding my success from the recruitment meeting, I decided it was time to close a loose end.

I followed my tracking beacon of light, which led me to a cave that held my target. The limestone was covered in moss, and the area was dense with trees.

There were no guards. However, there were a lot of snakes that stared at me as I entered through a small opening. They were resting on strategically placed stones covering every corner. It made me uneasy, but they did not move me.

The inside was not unpleasant. There was furniture and even decor that looked as if it belonged in your average temple. It was a comfortable place, but empty. There were no signs of any staff. Gods rarely take care of themselves —I'd certainly never seen it.

I found Keket looking into a telescope, surrounded by drawings of constellations. I almost didn't recognize the frog goddess, not flitting around or nervously shaking. She appeared a lot more natural in her own territory. She looked up and pushed away the scope. "The snakes told me of your approach."

Well, that explains why she didn't seem surprised.

"We need to speak," I said plainly.

"Yes…well…I didn't think this was a social call." She crossed her arms. "You're lucky you came when you did; I have little time left…"

"Can you even see stars at twilight?" I asked, both genuinely unsure and trying to establish some kind of rapport. The last time we had spoken, it was because I had summoned her. This time, I had just shown up using my power. I would be suspicious of a being who did that.

"With the right telescope, you can," she assured me. "You said we need to talk?"

"Right." I took a deep breath. "Well…time is running out on us. As you requested, I have returned now that I have assembled a team and a plan, and I'm here to recruit you to join us and take the fight to Apep."

She looked at the wall, not at me, when she replied, "I can't do that…My situation, I'm sorry, but it's changed."

I frowned. "What are you talking about?"

"My father spoke to me for the first time in over a decade to make it clear in no uncertain terms that should I lift a hand to help you; I won't live to pick up a sword." She was fidgeting again, as if my presence in her lair had triggered her earlier persona.

"I don't believe I understand," I said slowly. "This was always going to end in a fight. It had to. Surely your mother understood that when she started all this. I understand that interacting with him is terrifying. Trust me, I've only done it from afar, but still—"

"H-he wasn't supposed to see me coming!" she stuttered, cutting me off. "My mother reached out to you before my coming of age so we could prepare and strike…before all that."

Her tongue was doing the dramatic flicking again. "And even if I had confidence, it doesn't matter now. I can't leave." She gestured toward the entrance I had come in. "There's a force field." She saw my face and added, "Don't worry, it's just for me."

Guilt overtook me. She hadn't mentioned being suspicious of how he found out we were on his tail. I wasn't about to reveal it was my fault when I still needed her on our side. But it was because of me she was now trapped in her home. I wished I could help.

But I had neither the means nor really the time to investigate how to break a force field. Presumably, it would fall on its own once Apep was slain.

"Well," I pivoted. "While we would certainly appreciate you in our ranks, I understand your… predicament. Can I still count on you to be ready once he is displaced?"

"To take over as the goddess of darkness, you mean." She was looking at me again.

"Yes, someone must manage the night, and you are the heir; the prophecy makes that clear. I assume your mother has gone over all of this with you."

"What do you think would happen should I not do it?" she asked, uncrossing her arms.

I tilted my head slightly. "Not be the heir?" *What is she even asking?*

"I don't want to end up like him." Her voice was much softer now, missing any edge. "I have seen what darkness does to a heart." Her lips were quivering a bit.

Her doubt made sense now. My role in the prophecy was certainly scary. But the father I fought for, I would be proud if I ended up with even a fraction of his strength or power.

It is easy to accept a destiny that sets you up to be the hero.

I stepped closer, but slowly, so as not to startle her. I needed to use a delicate touch.

"Keket, it is not the darkness that makes your father corrupt. That is something he fell into on his own. He felt rejected; he fell in with voices that took advantage of something that was inside him."

Was this helping?

"But the night itself is not a bad thing," I assured her. We need it to balance the light. Taking charge of the dark does not mean you end up like him."

"You are just saying that," she insisted. "You don't even know me."

She's right, I don't.

"Well, should you not step up," I responded, "I honestly cannot guess what will happen. Perhaps Amun would choose someone else to take over. But without the same powers as you, the night sky could lose its way. It may change in color, or become weaker, maybe the stars would falter—"

"The stars?" she interrupted. "The stars could come to harm." Her eyes grew wide, but she was not quivering in fear anymore. Her voice was…protective?

I had not expected this to be so important to her.

"I mean, I don't believe there is anyone else with the same power…I assume you are… connected to them?"

She gestured for me to come over to her telescope, and I obliged. The conversation was taking an unexpected turn, but if this is what would work…

"I created a lot of the constellations you can see here." She moved the telescope lens around a bit, zooming in and then pointing at me to look.

I put my eye to the lens and quickly saw what she had pointed out. "Yes, that's Orion Sah, correct?"

She smiled. "I wanted something that could give people hope for rebirth. It's dedicated to Osiris. She loves by the way." Her voice portrayed a confidence I hadn't heard before.

I was not sure how the shape had anything to do with rebirth, but I wasn't about to push back against that. "It is quite beautiful," I said instead. It was. I wasn't familiar with its story. While some constellations had detailed tales within my father's library, many more had their name and shape recorded with no more information.

"Thank you. I am quite proud of my stars." She seemed thoughtful. "I didn't think about someone else managing my stars. Or worse, not managing them…"

I decided not to say anything for a minute. It seemed the lights in the sky were more convincing than anything I had managed to during this exchange, so maybe staying quiet was the better move.

"Alright, Bastet, I will step into my role when the time comes." Keket stood up straight.

I felt my muscles relax a bit. "I am happy to hear that."

We shook hands on it.

As I walked to the exit, I felt eyes watching me from the shadows.

Tawaret revealed herself, lowering the same hood I saw her wearing the first time we met in the temple. "Daughter of Ra."

"Bastet," I corrected her.

"I hope you understand now why I approached you the way you did."

I turned to face her. It was strange to see her again, in her territory instead of mine now. There were no more mysteries to uncover. For better or for worse, she was the reason I found out the truth.

"You were trying to protect your daughter," I affirmed. Under my breath, I muttered, "Perhaps I could've been a bit more polite about it."

"It is difficult to speak about certain matters when you are cursed by your previous partner not to do so," she contended.

I was right; she had been trying to tell me more when we met on the Solstice. How many curses did the god of chaos have wreaking havoc in our world?

"I tried everything I could before coming to you," she told me. "But yes, I would do anything to protect my daughter. Anyway, I wanted to say thank you for stepping up. I would accompany you in this fight, but I am also blocked by that accursed force field."

She glared in its direction. "I should've expected he would not fight fair."

I wasn't doing any of this for her, but I appreciated the sentiment anyway. "I understand," I replied. "And I would accept your thanks, but we have not yet won."

Her eyes grew suddenly dark. "Then I will instead wish you the best of luck in the fight. I hope you do not go in unprepared... It could be the death of us all."

I had pictured that too many times, I didn't want to again.

"Alright, I change my mind, a little faith would be appreciated," I said lightly, although I was only half joking. "You wound this goddesses pride."

"Do not take your pride with you to this fight," she responded. "Take your hope, your spirit, even your trust in destiny. But do not take your pride."

26

THE VASE

Time was running short, but I went to find my father, anyway. He was in his office, as I expected. The very place we had fought on this matter seemed so long ago.

He sat looking at a vase on his desk. "Do you remember making this?" he asked me as I walked in.

I smiled. "Sure, I do. I can't believe you kept it. Sekhmet and I must've been…five?"

Wepet-Renpet marked the start of the new year among our people. It was common for mortals to exchange water from the Nile during this time as a sign of best wishes for the next year.

Gods were often asked to bless this water. One year, as children, we decided that we too could get water blessed as a gift for our father.

So, first we worked together to craft a truly horrid vase out of some clay—my side was bumpier but level, and Sekhmet's side leaned a little bit. We both signed our names in hieroglyphs on each side, also an uneven match, as we didn't realize we were using two different shades of paint.

I remembered us arguing afterwards if we should throw the thing out and start over, but it was almost dinner time, and we had decided that was when we wanted to present it. Shu walked in, and then, after laughing at the quality of our work, offered to help us find someone to bless it.

My heart hurt a little while picturing his face. What if I never saw it again?

"I remember thinking, these girls of mine, they may bicker, but when they have a goal, it always gets done anyway," my father said softly.

I sat down. "Yes, we usually find a way to work together in the end." I thought back to our conversation at training.

"I'm glad you came to see me," he said. "I was hoping we'd have a moment to talk before the battle, but I wasn't sure you wanted to speak to me still. Things between us have been so difficult lately."

"That's part of why I came to find you, actually. I have been so angry…"

"And I understand it," my father clarified. "I do. I am not sure what I would do differently if given the chance, but…"

"You were trying to protect me," I finished. "I know. And I didn't like that at first, but…I just came back from speaking with Keket."

"Oh?" My father seemed surprised. "Your sister informed me that you had spoken to her a week or two ago, but that you weren't sure if she would come through in the end."

I nodded. "Yes, I went to confirm that she is ready."

"And?"

"And she's so afraid, Father. We both come from ancient gods whose existence is so tied to the very basics of human life. And I thought that would make us alike. Maybe even in a way, Sekhmet and I aren't alike, our connections to the sun and to the stars. But he's just left her with this terrible legacy, and…" I couldn't forget the fear in her eyes when she talked about inheriting his wickedness.

I felt myself starting to ramble. "I just came to say I'm sorry. I could've ended up with a lot less than a father who cares so much that maybe he's just a bit, I suppose you could say, overprotective."

My father smiled, and his voice was thick with emotion as he spoke. "I am very happy to hear you say that. I am sorry for Keket; it cannot have been easy to live in that shadow. Thoth and I tried to reach out to her mother several times throughout the years, but it was always you she needed to speak with, so it seems."

"Oh, I don't think she's doing it for me. She's doing it because she really likes the stars." I laughed. It sounded silly to say the fate of our world lay in the balance because a snake god's daughter wanted to keep the stars shining in the sky. But I was grateful for it.

For a moment, I reveled in the moment's peace. The tension had finally dissipated between us.

I need to tell him the truth.

"Father, I need to tell you something." I held my hand up to the spot the amulet used to it. "In order to call Heka…"

"You sacrificed the amulet." There was no emotion in his response, simply a recitation of a fact.

"I'm so sorry…"

"I wish you had not, but I appreciate you telling me. I do not wish to go into tomorrow's battle with any resentment, on both our sides. Do not worry on it."

I breathed a sigh of relief.

"But daughter, I also have to use this time to prepare you, if I can. You are unfamiliar with war," my father said, his voice firm.

"Yes, I am certainly inexperienced; that has been established," I replied, working hard not to get on edge and to hold on to our newfound understanding.

He leaned forward a bit.

"I do not say this to look down on you or lecture you; I am saying this because while I am grateful you have been spared thus far from the losses that occur in battle, that may not be the case after tomorrow."

I blinked. What is he trying to say? Did he think I was unaware of the risks? Yes, I'd never fought myself. But I knew more about death than most gods. I saw it every night in Duat. I felt it daily in the loss of my mother.

"I will tell you what I told your sister. My duty is to this family. I created you in a desperate time, to save the world and myself from a great darkness. You did not ask to be created, but you have done your role well for many years. Tomorrow, Bastet, you are not my defender. Do you understand?" His voice was solemn, and he was looking me in the eye as he asked.

"No, I'm not really sure I do," I answered truthfully.

"I am not an all-powerful ancient god when I am in the underworld. Without the light of the sun to fuel my weapons and my life force, I will barely be up to par with some of the half-gods under your sister's employ."

I was getting worried. "Perhaps you should just stay back then," I suggested. "We have a good group. I'm honestly impressed by how many people even said yes—"

"No, I started this fight. I will be there for its end." His voice was firm.

"Alright, then why are you telling me all this?" I furrowed my brow.

"I am telling you this, daughter, because I want you to remember that tomorrow, you are not my defender. I am yours. You are to defend the sun, you are to defend your brother, but do not concern yourself with what happens to me, alright?"

I shook my head. "How am I supposed to promise that?"

"If I perish, Bastet, someone else has to step up and raise the sun, the same way you asked Keket tonight if she would stand in for her father."

My whole body felt cold, as if ice had been injected into my veins.

I was beginning to hate this conversation. "Yes, but Keket is the better person for that job. She has no evil in her heart and loves the stars. That's not—you're not, talking about the same thing." My voice was starting to shake.

"I have already discussed it with Amun," my father explained. "If Apep is slain, he will unlock your powers. Even if something happens to me. And when I perish, the light powers will go to you. Someone needs to be able to rise with the sun. We cannot let the world fall into darkness."

Why would he discuss this with him? It's NOT going to happen!

"No!" I exclaimed. I threw out my arms, as if I could physically repel the thought away. "I don't want them. Why not Shu or Sekhmet?"

"Because Shu takes after his mother, he inherited no light powers from me. And that makes you technically my firstborn, as you came to be in this world mere minutes before your sister.

Sekhmet and I had heard about this, of course. But the fact only existed as something to be used in a joke if I wanted her to listen to me, or she wanted me to feel old.

It wasn't supposed to mean anything.

It doesn't mean anything, because I'm not doing it.

If I were destined to inherit some light powers, why couldn't Heka have unlocked those for me instead of this nonsense with the all-seeing eye? No one would look at me and think I could step up and be the god of the sun. Ridiculous!

"I am not saying it will happen, daughter." His voice was a bit gentler. "But if it does, I need you to be ready."

"I'm not," I insisted, fighting off tears. I was already the star of this prophecy. I had stepped up to it. I was doing my part. This was too much.

"You are, you always have been. You are no longer a child, even if I have only just realized it now. And…Ptah will be a wonderful husband for you someday."

My face turned red, not expecting the sudden tonal shift. "You know about that…?" I wiped some moisture from my face.

"My dear Bastet, everyone knew before you. The point is, I am not leaving you alone. You will have him, your sister, and, in a few days, your brother. So please do not be afraid."

"I will try my best." I meant it this time.

"That's all I could hope for."

27

NEPHTHYS

And so the sisters of Ra had assembled a team. Or perhaps I should say, I assembled a team that reported to my sister.

I did not mind that Sekhmet had taken charge—it was natural to her. After our disastrous first session, she had all but ordered me to focus on locating Apep. We would practice different ways to land a blow afterward, but if I couldn't even find Apep, there was no point in worrying about the rest. The rest, she claimed, would just be distracting.

I could not correct her. Despite my practice, I still could only locate items and people. While my locating powers seemed to improve—which was good—I still felt a bit like I was playing hide-and-seek whenever I asked someone to practice with me.

Ptah had volunteered to be the "primary target". I hated that he called it that, but he was just excited to be involved. I would search for him in dark hallways, forests of figs, and long stretches of desert. Every time, he would say something quippy like "I quite like being chased" or "you're right, it is hard to hide from you."

Something had changed in him since I had told him of my returned feelings. It was as if he

218

were a freer version of himself. As if now that all was in the open, he could say whatever crossed his mind.

Luckily, Sekhmet approved of the daggers when I finally had a chance to show them to her.

She gushed over the craftsmanship even more than I had, although hers was more practical. "I should've thought of this earlier. Of course, Ptah could make you something. When this is over, I am commissioning him to make weapons for my entire troop, I swear."

It was nice to see her excited.

"These will fit you perfectly. They are lightweight, can be concealed if needed, and sharp enough to do some real damage." She held one up to the light.

"Sister, I must warn you, however, that no weapon relies more on close-up combat than a dagger."

The prophecy didn't exactly imply this battle could be won with a distant arrow or by throwing my spear, so I had accepted this.

"Then teach me close-up combat?" I asked.

I tried not to remember the records I had read in the library of those who had tried the same approach to fight Apep.

I will get as close as it takes.

On my remaining rides through Duat, I practiced with the daggers as she instructed. I brought on a training dummy and focused on stabbing in all the spots she told me I should focus on.

I practiced general sparring with Henet, who was not as talented as Sekhmet or her soldiers, but still a better use of my time than staring out in the deep waters. Occasionally, other crew members gave me advice on my form.

We were not in his territory, we were on our own. Apep would lose all his leverage if he attacked us now.

What my sister and I had both left unspoken was the fact that fighting a giant snake could not be practiced on a field or with a dummy. I had picked up a book on reptile anatomy from the library and was studying where the equivalent spots (the neck, the heart, etc.) would be located. But all the practice in the world with a human-shaped target wouldn't prepare me fully.

Two days before the deadline, I grew restless. It felt like I was forgetting something—as if somewhere in the world was a guide to defeating an ancient, chaotic god, and I had checked off many of the steps, but accidentally skipped one.

When I discussed this with Sekhmet over dinner, I expected her to be annoyed by the questioning and brush it off. Instead, she looked at me closely. "Well, one of your main jobs was recruiting. Do you feel that you have asked everyone to join who should be with us?"

It was a good thing to consider. I had not gone into the meeting with any concrete goals, only hopes that we could put together the best team possible to fight Apep. That was vague and undefined.

"Would you say there is something we are missing?" She prodded forward.

Had she already thought about this? Why hadn't she said something sooner?

I thought through the types of fighters we had—ancient gods, young gods, half-gods. There were a variety of powers of different natural elements, and those with more physicality to their powers. But...

"We don't have a healer," I realized. How had I missed that? Every good battalion needed a healer. There were team members with minor healing powers, sure, but no one whose domain was truly that of healing.

"Yes, I had begun to think of that," Sekhmet said.

I frowned. "Why didn't you say something sooner? I could have been working on it." Or she could have tried herself, but saying so did not feel particularly conducive to the conversation, so I kept that thought to myself.

"It was recent," she replied. "And I wasn't sure how to present the idea to you."

"You know someone?" I asked, my ears perking up in excitement.

"Well, we are related to one..." I wasn't used to her beating around the bush this much in a conversation; her voice trailed off as if it were a question.

"Our mother was a healer, yes, but she's not exactly here to help…"

Sekhmet rolled her eyes. "I know that, sister. But she is not the only one in her family line who rules over that domain."

I stared off, pondering for a moment, before realization hit me. "You mean… Nephthys?"

It's been a long time since I've heard that name.

Our aunt had not spoken to anyone in our family since the day my mother died. She blamed my father, and by extension all his children, for her sister's death. This was not an unreasonable assumption. No one really blamed her for feeling this way. My father used to try and send letters in the beginning.

We children had even written one together for the New Year one time. We were still quite young and knew our handwriting was nothing to be impressed by, so we dictated the message to Shu. I did not remember the exact wording, but it was basically a summary of our lessons and life as a whole, best wishes for the new year, and stating we wanted to see more of her.

She never wrote back.

"Why would she help us?" I asked, honestly baffled. I would have never considered reaching out to her on my own.

"She does not like the memories we are associated with," Sekhmet responded. "But we are still family. We still share blood with her. I do not think she would want us to come to harm."

While I was sure she did not literally wish us ill, I wasn't convinced she would want any kind of direct involvement in a fight. I didn't remember much about her exact powers, although I could assume they were like our mother's.

"Do you even know how to contact her?" I asked, still not convinced.

"We have the address, we have always had to send our messenger birds, but we don't need that…"

"We…don't?"

"Would your all-seeing eye not work for this? You have told me the requirements: a strong connection, either by blood or emotion, and that you have had to see the person before, yes?" Sekhmet pointed out. "Yes, it had been a long time since we saw our aunt, but we did meet her." It should follow the qualifications."

"I mean…" I wanted to disagree, but truthfully, it made sense. While everyone I had used the power on so far was someone I had seen actually unlocking it, Heka had not mentioned anything about a time frame.

I shrugged. "Alright, I suppose, I will try. But…don't get your hopes up or anything."

Sekhmet nodded, looking pleased with herself.

I closed my natural eye and began to search for Nephthys. I did not have any fresh memories to work with, so I reached back into the past. It was blurry, but I could see enough.

I found a mental image from before she left us—of a time as children we had walked along the Nile, and she told me about the types of fish. The memory was hazy, but I could still see her eyes, so similar in shape and color to my mother's.

I focused on that, her blue eyes, and the rest of her appearance filled in the blanks—her straight and long black hair, her anklet that matched my mother's. I don't think my conscious mind could have explained what she looked like, but now the image was clear.

My mind pulled away from the past as the memory faded like smoke, and I was brought back to the present.

My tracking light led me away from the temple and into the desert. It was moving fast, but I kept up, the landscape rushing past.

And then it found her. A small cottage along the water, clearly some walk from Heliopolis. Reeds surrounded it, with no other buildings in sight. She was sitting on a bench outside the cabin, reading something.

"I…can see where she is," I exclaimed, blinking and returning my vision to what lay in front of me.

Sekhmet grinned. "How interesting… it seems that power is quite useful after all."

I hadn't expected that to work. "I still don't think she will help us, but…"

"But either way, we really need a healer," Sekhmet finished. "It's not a good idea to go into this fight without one."

I hated how often she was right. "Fine…I will go and…say something to her, I have no idea what, but…will you come with me?"

"I can, but I'm pretty sure you were always her favorite." She sounded slightly embarrassed.

"Strange to hear you so humble," I noted, finding her admission humorous, although I had no idea if it was true. My memories of our aunt seemed to be fainter than hers.

"I simply pay attention to those that like me and those that do not," she huffed. "But it would be useful to see these powers of yours in use anyway, so I will accompany you. Shall we go?"

I looked at the sundial on the wall. "My tracker does not tell me the exact distance. I am not sure how far we will have to go. Do you want to risk that?"

"We do not have much time left until our mission, sister. We will just have to be fast."

I pushed away my plate and stood up. "Alright then, let's do this."

28

THE LETTER

Other than the vaults with Ptah, I had spent most of my quests and explorations alone. It felt kind of nice having someone to explore with, especially because this particular expedition involved family dynamics and history I would rather not face alone.

"I just realized I have met more people and traveled more outside our palace than in the rest of my years combined," I noted as we exited the main entrance.

"And how is the outside world?" my sister asked, amused. She was, of course, the opposite of me—always on the move, tracking down criminals and rebels.

"It definitely has its charms," I replied. "But I can also appreciate the peace of the underworld a bit more."

"This mission will be my first time seeing that," Sekhmet pointed out.

I hadn't thought about that before. There were few things I was more experienced in than her. But navigating the underworld? It was not comfortable, as there was always a risk of danger, but it did feel familiar.

"I'll be sure to give you the expert tour." I oriented myself to the tracking light, the same way one might find north on a compass. "This way," I pointed.

"Perhaps I should have summoned Heka myself after all," Sekhmet noted, following me. "I might have been able to unlock some kind of power myself."

"Why didn't you?" I wondered.

"You've had more time to train. I have no idea what my power could be. If I got something complicated or potentially dangerous, it could actually be more of a liability than anything else."

I felt a bit guilty. If I had told her sooner, she might have had time to do so. "But even when I had the power, you weren't ready to move forward. You could have gone to Heka immediately, before Apep instituted this deadline."

"I was concerned that if I showed too much enthusiasm, you would end up getting hurt. Which of course, we barely avoided in the end."

I wanted to argue that I might have had more patience if she'd agreed to train me, but truth be told, I couldn't be sure. I had let the impatience in my heart rule over anything else.

As we left Heliopolis, the road started to get rougher, and the trees more frequent. After about an hour of walking, I realized I was the farthest from the city I had ever traveled.

"One of the first things I'm going to do once we're free," I told Sekhmet, "Is travel somewhere that takes a whole day to get to. I don't even care if it's someplace interesting. I'll pick a line on a map, and walk until I'm so far I'd never make it back by dawn. And then I'll sleep if I'm tired, but it will be on my terms."

"Sure, or you could also actually pick somewhere interesting," she teased. "Otherwise, you may end up in the wilderness and need to be rescued again."

I laughed. "What about you? What are you going to do with your freedom? I don't mean big picture; I mean something small you've always wanted to do."

She didn't respond immediately, instead adjusting the weapon on her belt. "Me? I'd just enjoy a day when I'm not expected to do anything at all."

I raised an eyebrow. "I wouldn't have guessed that." I thought she loved the daily grind.

"Just like you, I spend the majority of my time awake working for our father. I do not do it with him, but don't forget that I am stuck doing his busywork until you guys reach the land. And I am proud to do it. Truly. But I do not have an identity…outside the work."

That much I could understand. We were both defined by our father from the moment we were born. I had always assumed that since Sekhmet at least got to speak to other gods, not travel the same route day after day, she must feel freer.

I was learning that there is more than one way to be stuck.

After another half-hour of walking, the surrounding environment finally resembled what I had seen in my vision. Good, if we move fast, we shouldn't have too much trouble getting back by dawn.

"We are close," I told Sekhmet, pointing to a cottage in front of us. "Do you have any idea what to say?"

"Not particularly," she admitted. "But we'll figure it out."

The cottage was very cozy. I had never seen a god living in such a small place. There did not appear to be any staff, although there was some evidence of a partner, based on the size of the outdoor furniture and some clothes hung up on a line.

Nephthys was sitting on a bench on the edge of her property, which was surrounded by tall purple flowers I didn't recognize. She was knitting and did not look up until we were merely a few feet away. "My nieces," she noted, finally looking up.

"We…expected you to be more surprised," Sekhmet noted, glancing at me.

She set down her knitting tools on the table next to her. "You recently turned eighteen. I knew I would see you shortly after."

She remembered our birthday? I was not sure whether to feel touched that she'd remembered a date for so long or hurt that every year the day came across her mind, and yet she didn't reach out to us.

She really did look so much like our mother. Her hair was styled differently, but just as in my vision, her hazel eyes made them appear more like twins than my sister and me, who actually were.

"How is it you knew?" I asked.

"Follow me inside," she replied, not answering my question.

I looked at Sekhmet, who shrugged. There wasn't much else to do but follow.

Our aunt was certainly not a minimalist. Inside, while certainly not as prestigious looking as a temple, there was decor everywhere. Every inch of wall was covered in a painting or nature, or some kind of knit design. There was so much color, I felt the need to blink.

She gestured for us to sit at her dining room table, a small cedar structure with four chairs. "Would you like something to drink?"

"I'm sure whatever you have is fine." My answers were stilted, the awkwardness in the air almost palpable.

"I'll pour you some hibiscus tea." She got up and pulled out some cups for all three of us.

"You like collecting?" Sekhmet said as a way of conversation, taking in all the art.

"I enjoy looking at things pleasing to the eye," she answered, pouring in the last cup and then bringing them to the table.

She set down the cups, and the slight floral smell of the tea reached my nose. "I assume you two are still on a timetable?"

She remembered that as well.

"I nodded. Yes, we must do our best to be back by dawn, lest we fall asleep on your doorstep." I looked for a sundial, but it was difficult to locate anything in the clutter.

"We do not need to keep our pretenses for too long then," she responded, sitting down. "I understand you must have disdain for me."

"I wouldn't say that," Sekhmet said quietly.

I agreed. "It…hurt to not get any replies to our letters," I admitted, "But we kept writing them because we hoped that maybe someday you'd want to see us again."

I watched Nephthys' eyes drift over to a pile in the room as she next spoke. Were those the very letters? "Yes, writing back might have been the kinder thing to do. I just didn't want to give you false hope. I have no plans of ever returning to Heliopolis. And I wasn't sure you could even make it out this far with your limitations."

"It would have been nice to at least hear from you," I said quietly, gripping my hand around my teacup and feeling the slight heat.

"It wounds me how much I can see her in your eyes," she murmured. It was telling that she felt that way, as I had been thinking the same about our mother. All of us were here because of her.

Death was so rare in the world of the gods that it wasn't really a normal way to react. Mortals had ceremonies, funeral rites they performed, and different ways to honor the dead as time went by. We didn't have such practices or rituals. My father had asked us if we wanted a funeral, but at the time, I had never even heard of one and had no idea how it could help.

There was also the fact that mortals could rely on an eventual reunion—should they both pass the mortal tests of Anubis, that is. But that was a powerful motivator for them to live a good life, so they could earn an afterlife together.

But gods did not have such a promise. While we were told the resting place of the gods existed, most of us would never reach there. The mourning did not have an expiration date. Our only comfort was the belief that she was at peace there.

It was for that reason that no one had ever come here and dragged Nephthys home. Amun normally would've never allowed someone to simply abandon their domain the way she had. Especially since with the passing of my mother, there was one less ancient healing god out in the world.

Sekhmet broke the moment of silence with a cough. "Listen, we are here to ask you something." She told her all about Apep, how he had taken Shu, and how soon we would have to face off with him. "We have been working hard to recruit a team of gods to give us a fighting chance," she finished. "But we are close to our final day with no healer to speak of."

I've been the one doing all the recruiting, I thought, somewhat spitefully. But this last one had been her idea after all.

"The likelihood of someone getting injured is unfortunately high," I added. "And there is no better than you to keep us safe."

"Poor Shu," she responded. "I have missed him as well."

As well? Was she admitting to having missed us?

"But I cannot help you," she said firmly, crushing hope that had slowly been growing inside me. "I'm sorry."

"Why not?" Sekhmet demanded, looking just as hurt as I was.

She pointed to a small portrait of her and her partner, some kind of wolf god. "I have a family of my own now." She touched her stomach. "I am with child."

It must be new, as she was not showing yet, but I had no reason to believe she was lying. "Oh."

Her voice was apologetic. "Under different circumstances, I can't tell you how I might have responded. But such is the state you have found me."

"But you said you knew we were coming," I pointed out. "That, for whatever reason, you expected we'd be coming once we turned of age."

She stood up. "Only because your mother asked me to hold something for you until then." She went to the other room briefly, returning with two envelopes stuffed with something. She handed one to each of us.

"What is this?" Sekhmet asked, turning the envelope over and rubbing her hand on the ink containing her first name on the front. I recognized our mother's handwriting.

"My sister, before she went on that expedition that would be death...she gave me these. She made me promise that should anything happen to her, I would hold on to them. That once you turned eighteen, you would need whatever was inside. Don't worry, I have never opened them. The messages are for you and you alone."

I was full of both a desire to rip open the letter and a fear of what it would feel like afterward, having no message from my mother that I hadn't yet read. Despite the fact this letter had been completely unknown to us up until now, there was something oddly comforting about seeing there was something new my mother could tell me.

But Sekhmet was already reading hers at that point, and curiosity ran supreme.

Dear Bastet:

As I scribble these words, I feel in my heart they may be among the last I may ever pen. It would have been simpler to write you and your sister something together, but my knowledge of your hearts tells me there are different things you need in a final message from your mother.

I do not imagine that the sheer length of immortality makes sense to you yet. Before you and your sister were born, I had already lived centuries in this world. I knew your father for a long time, since almost the beginning—but it took years for us to understand what partnership meant for beings with infinite power.

Eventually, every day is the same in the world when you have seen all there is to see. That was when we decided to have Shu. And oh, how the world became fresh once again. A new generation breathed fresh life into the gods.

I say all this to tell you something important. My death is not a tragedy. The biggest fear I have is that you will feel guilty over the risks I took for this family.

Remember this—you did not choose to be born. A child exists because two people take action to create life. And you two, you were made, in part, to save your father. When he told me what Amun had proposed, I hated the idea of placing such a heavy destiny on two young kids.

But I loved him, and the family we had started. Therefore, I agreed, and you were born.

The moment I saw you, you were not just an idea—you were real, and I felt the weight of what we'd done. You were essentially cursed, and we had brought you into the world accepting that was your fate.

Every moment since, I have been chasing your freedom.

If you're reading this, it means I did not succeed. It means I am among the few gods to move to the next plane. But I am at rest, I am at peace. I do not worry about how Anubis will judge my soul, and I do not want you to worry either, do you understand?

While I have failed, you are about to enter the fight for your freedom on your own. I will not leave you stranded in this battle. Your father should have given you a bracelet I made with the help of my sister.

As clever as you are, you have likely accepted the fact that you would find out how to open it only when the time is right.

The time is now. With this letter, I give you my final gift, the key to the vial that can save a life.

Use it sparingly. Use it well.

I have faith that you will win.

Watch over your sister; she does not express her love as openly as you do. Learn from her strength, and let her learn from your heart.

Remember that I love you.
Mother

29

PREPARING THE MIND

I held the letter to my heart, tears streaming down my face. I did not fight them; this was a moment that I wanted to feel. I was so grateful these words existed. I did not realize how much I needed them. How much I needed to hear that she believed in us!

I took out the key and placed it in the small hole in the ankh. It clicked open immediately. Inside was a tiny vial, glowing with green liquid.

Sekhmet reached out and squeezed my hand —an unexpectedly tender gesture that made me wonder what her letter might have contained. Mother had written them differently for each of us, after all.

"Your mother always was talented with her words," Nephthys remarked.

"Thank you for holding onto these," Sekhmet said quietly.

"Of course. I wish I could do more, but…I will not risk the life growing inside me. And this battle you prepare to fight…well, I am sure you do not need me to tell you the level of danger."

At least she didn't say "good luck."

I wiped my eyes. "Would you at least consider coming to visit us? When it's all over, and we are free?"

She took a deep breath. "I will consider it."

Trusting that was likely the best we would get, we excused ourselves to begin the journey back.

"You can sleep here if you like," she offered. "I'm sure you are cutting it close."

"I think Father would be nervous if we were to disappear so close to our mission," Sekhmet said. "We didn't tell him we were coming. But thank you."

"I hope we see you again," I added.

She did not reply.

The walk home was much quieter. We walked faster, and it felt like there was too much to say—and no words for the emotions conveyed in the letters.

Even Sekhmet was out of breath when we reached the door to the residential chambers. "Good evening, sister. Use the remaining time to prepare yourself, but please do not be late. We leave at twilight."

There was no ride to Duat today. Father had employed some other gods to fill in my task for this one day—we needed all the time possible before dawn for our attack.

Of course, there was a risk. Apep could take his army and capture the sun instead of fighting us. But that is why my father would not be joining the battle immediately. He would remain on the ship until it was clear that he was true to his word —he would face us for the life of my brother.

It was mere minutes before twilight when I snuck into Ptah's sleeping chamber.

I'd never been in this room before, even though I'd spent plenty of time in this temple. But there was no doubt I was in the right place. Paintings covered the walls, some his, some from ancient artists. I noticed one of my own in the corner, which was touching.

It felt strange to be in this place that was entirely his. But I had a feeling he wouldn't mind.

He rose at my entry. "Bastet, isn't the battle about to begin? Did Sekhmet really let you free?" He wiped sleep from his eyes.

I laughed. "She doesn't know I'm here. I needed to see you." I went and sat beside him on the bed. Even fully clothed, I was surprised by how intimate the moment felt. My heart began to race.

"Are you afraid?" he asked, softly. He put his arm around me.

I wanted to say something brave and strong, to claim I wasn't afraid at all. But Ptah was not someone I could lie to. "A little. But I also accept that this is what history has destined, regardless of the result."

"That is admirable. It takes much greater courage to be scared and do something anyway."

I smiled halfheartedly. "Thank you, but I feel it is more about just being realistic for once. My sister would be proud."

"No, I mean it," he insisted. "This all started because you weren't afraid to hear out a random goddess who approached you from afar. Everything you've learned, everything you have overcome… I do not think many of us can say we have put in even half that amount of effort as a deity."

I grabbed his hand. "Yes, that is where it started. But surely you can tell it's about more than just that now."

"Oh?" He linked his fingers around mine, and the warmth was comforting in the cool night. "Tired of sleeping all day, I assume?"

I blushed. "Well, I've realized there's someone I'd like to spend more time with, actually."

"Have I met him?" Ptah feigned confusion.

"You are close with him actually," I teased.

"Oh, right, yes, I believe you owe that man another date?" He winked.

I squeezed his hand. "Well, then he'll just have to stick around."

We sat in companionable silence for a moment. I closed my eyes and tried to freeze this picture in my mind; in case I didn't get to experience anything like this again. In case it was the last time.

"Can I tell you another reason I am doing this? "I asked, once my eyes had opened again.

He nodded.

I told him about the young girl in Duat, the one who was at peace because she was on the way to being reunited with her beloved. How death itself was welcome to her, because it meant they could be together again.

"At the time, it did not make sense to me," I reflected. "She was so young, and mortal life is so short. But…I understand now. Because, should my existence cease tomorrow—or should the sky itself bleed red—somehow, some way, we will be reunited. If not in this life, then whatever comes next. No matter the result of this battle, this is not the end for us."

Ptah used his other hand to lightly cup my face. "Of course, it is not the end. You will return victorious, and the day shall be yours. No, if you let me share it with you, it will be ours."

While his voice was sincere, I wondered if he believed that or just hoped for it.

We kissed, lightly at first and then more urgently. My face felt flushed with heat. The impropriety of it all… But I don't think anyone would have faulted me for having this moment before I risked my life.

After a few moments had passed, the reality of time struck me again. "I must go," I whispered. "Please wait for me."

"As long as it takes."

30

SETTING SAIL

The moment I stepped outside, the grim reality of what I was about to do replaced all the warmth in my heart.

I was walking toward the fight with the god of chaos.

There was no more time to practice, no more late-night trips to the library, no more soldiers to recruit or allies to convince.

There was only the fight.

When I joined the battalion, the other gods we had recruited were already suiting up in armor and polishing their weapons. Sekhmet squinted suspiciously at me, but to my surprise, said nothing about my late arrival.

I pulled out my daggers and coated them again with the poisonous flower mix, just in case, although I had already done so the day before. Normally, I would sharpen my spear before a battle, but the daggers' edges were still pristine.

It didn't matter—I just needed something to do with my hands, anything to keep them from shaking.

Sekhmet's soldiers arrived shortly afterwards. I had not seen them since my failed attempt to tackle the polar bear half-god, and the memory made me flush with embarrassment.

Are they nervous about following me into battle after seeing my fighting skills?

I forced myself to take several deep breaths. You only need to land the finishing blow. You only need to land the finishing blow. The Finishing blow… I kept repeating it, hoping it would help.

I searched the faces of the soldiers to see if they were whispering about me or looked afraid.

They were serious and focused, barely talking to each other. Some were praying. I considered saying something to build their confidence in me or maybe even thanking them. But I decided it would only be interrupting whatever their pre-battle routine was.

But I needed to get up. I could not sit still and stew in my thoughts or repeat mantras.

I started walking over to Sekhmet when I noticed a familiar face near the ship.

"What are you doing here, Henet?" I asked, startled. I had not invited her to my recruitment meetings or mentioned her to my family. For one, I had assumed she would stay on Ra's ship. For two, I had not invited anyone young or inexperienced. I was asking gods to risk their lives; no reason to make the expedition even riskier.

She smiled, looking up from the rudder of the ship. "You thought you could sail without me?"

"I mean, I'm happy to see you…it's just you serve my father's crew, not mine. I hate the idea of you in danger for a quest that was supposed to be my own." I bit my lip. Who had told her where we were meeting?

"Bastet, your friendship was the reason I stayed on the Meneset's crew so long. My parents told me I could move on years ago to begin my full duties. Of course I would be here."

It was a touching notion, but it brought a sense of guilt—another person who had quietly put their life on hold because of me, waiting for me to step into my prophesied destiny.

"I'll get Ptah to build you an amazing temple," I promised, coughing away the lump raised in my throat. He wouldn't mind if I was signing him up for something.

She winked. "I'll hold you to that."

I turned away then, wanting to refocus my mind, but found it difficult. I started to walk to Sekhmet, but my hands were shaking again. All lives were valuable—but I now had so many personal connections to the people fighting this fight. It had been easier when it was just me risking my own life—now I knew so many people I couldn't bear to lose.

"Bastet, will you confirm the location?" my sister asked when I finally finished reaching her. While we checked earlier, I don't want to take any chances. The mortal soldiers can't move as quickly as us, and I do not want to waste any time changing course."

I had half expected her to impart some kind of emotional greeting, but I was relieved when she didn't. I was barely holding back my emotions already.

"Yes, I will get started," I replied.

"By the way, I found a healer," she added. "I clearly continue to surpass expectations, hoping you can as well."

I rolled my eyes, even though it was a relief. She left me to get ready.

Despite all my practice, I still hadn't been able to locate Apep with the eye. I had never seen him. Although Heka claimed it was possible, he hadn't exactly given me any guidance. Maybe my feelings of hate toward him simply paled in comparison to the love and desire to protect my loved ones.

Instead, I looked for Shu once again. It had crossed my mind he was keeping him somewhere separate—but if a fight was what he wanted, that did not make sense. I had to trust that there was no trap waiting when both parties wanted to face off. And if there was a trap? Well, for my brother, I'd walk in willingly.

Meanwhile, Sekhmet was addressing her troops.

"All of you have gathered here today to cement yourself as an important part of history. Not all answered the call, but you have, and my sister and I thank you for your service."

There was a bit of polite clapping. I found myself distracted from my work.

"You do not just join us today to fight to free my brother, although my family owes you a debt of gratitude for doing so. You are helping us fight chaos itself—to protect the very nature of light and darkness." As she spoke, she gestured to the stars in the sky.

I was struck by the power behind her words. Her audience ranged from the weak half-god to deities with powers we had never seen. Yet they all looked at her, entranced.

"I have faith not only in the diverse range of powers and abilities of those who stand before me, but in the spirit and determination we bring to this fight. We do not come with our weapons alone; we come harnessing the embodiment of all that is light and good. It is for that reason that we will be victorious!" She raised her sword toward the sky.

This time, the applause was thunderous.

Being as young as she was and without her full powers, I had always assumed people only listened to my sister because of her lineage. It was at that moment that I realized she was so much more than that. She didn't just have courage and our father's shrewdness—she had the rare ability to win over people's hearts.

Still, if she read my thoughts, she would be yelling at me to focus on locating Shu. I closed my eyes, more determined this time. It took a few minutes of shifting through darkness and fog within my mind. There was no light at our destination.

But then, I saw his face, and the small light of guidance appeared in the corner of my eye. "Sekhmet," I called, "I have found him."

31

THE UNDERWATER LAIR

I did not think Duat could get any darker. But as we approached Apep's lair, I did not need my eye to pulse or search for the thread of light. The stars of the souls at peace could not pierce the void here.

I glanced at Sekhmet, concerned. I did not fear for us—we had our cat abilities to guide us. The other major deities had their own strong senses to rely on. But how would the lower-powered soldiers fare in such low visibility?

We rode in complete darkness for what was likely only a minute, though it felt like an hour. Everyone fell silent. "Sister," I said quietly. "Should we turn around?"

"Are we still on the path to Shu?"

"Yes," I confirmed, still seeing a small, glowing dot in the further periphery of my vision.

"Then we carry on. I do not believe all of Apep's army has perfect night vision. Perhaps the demons he controls, but not those with sentience. Eventually, there will be a light source."

Her theory proved correct—slowly, faint red torches appeared along the path—sparse at first, then closer together—until we neared a dock. There was no land here; the dock itself was forged of metal, secured with massive anchors to keep it from drifting in the underworld's waters. I recognized the ship that had once approached my father and tethered ours alongside it, along with several other vessels of similar design.

In the middle of the dock loomed a huge titanium door that faced downward. The realization sent a shiver through me—the entire base was underwater. This explained why it was so difficult to see from afar. There was no structure to see, no sounds that could be heard.

When our ship stilled, I narrowed my eyes. I had expected a barrage of guards, maybe even swarms of arrows to fall from the sky as we landed. They knew we were coming. But before I could ask my sister, the demons attacked.

They had not been waiting on the dock where we could strike first. They were hiding in the boats nearby and took advantage of the seconds it took for us to get bearings on the new location.

The soldiers rolled out first, bum-rushing the demons with melee weapons. I blindly went to follow, but Sekhmet shoved me back. "Do not lose sight of our mission, sister. I will not lose you to the front lines."

I nodded meekly, searching for another route to get inside the lair.

"I will cover you," Anuket promised. She strung a fiery arrow into her bow. "The demons are very single-minded, but should they get distracted and notice you, I will take them down from here."

"Thank you," I said, my voice hollow.

But my feet did not comply. It was as if an invisible force was holding me in place.

I tried not to listen to the clash of weapons or the sound of bodies falling into the water. Instead, I let all the sounds get muffled.

This was what my father had tried to warn me of—this exact moment. The moment I truly understood, that I could die.

I had read about war in the records; heard stories from other gods. I had imagined how I might feel over and over these past few days, but the reality was more intense, terrifying than I could ever have pictured.

I remembered my failed scuffle with the crocodiles. You couldn't even call it a fight. Neither their teeth nor my spear had reached any kind of target. But I failed at even that. How can I do this?

But then I saw Henet, sprinting forward with the other soldiers, no fear evident in her eyes. I could not afford to be afraid. I gripped my daggers tight, thinking of Ptah, who was surely worrying for me. I thought of my brother inside the lair. I glanced over at my sister beside me. There were too many who depended on me.

The invisible bind holding me shattered. I ran, leaning into every one of my cat instincts to dash quickly and quietly. I did not let myself look at any demon, only caught flashes of them in my peripheral vision. I stopped only to thrust open the bulkhead door and jump inside.

Standing in a small open hallway, the noise was somewhat deafened by the water-tight heaviness of the door.

I walked down the hallway slowly, lit with more of the red torches, brighter when protected from the outside elements.

It seemed most of the guards had gone outside to fight. The hallway split ahead, and I was grateful for the all-seeing eye, as there were no clear signs of what lay in either direction. I followed the pulsing light to the left, trusting it to keep guiding my way.

All my senses were on high alert. My ears twitched at every sound; my eyes searched for any sense of danger. Strange scents filled my nostrils, but at least I did not smell blood.

Every second felt like a minute and although every step moved me forward, it was not enough.

Finally, I saw a group of live human guards patrolling a large-looking room that seemed to be Apep's war room. My heart lurched, and I instinctively gripped the daggers tighter. I was able to slip through the shadows, unseen. That was not my destination yet.

The light was getting stronger. I was closer.

The walls grew plain, dingy—a sign I had reached the dungeon. I could tell I was at the entrance when I finally saw another closed door for the first time. Two demons stood before it, holding swords. I noticed one of them had a chain of keys hanging off his belt.

I couldn't put it off any longer; I was going to have to fight. There was no one else to wield an arrow or protect me. But I could not crash in— there were two of them, and one of me. I pulled off a chain-mail glove and threw it wildly in the opposite direction down the hall.

One of them took the bait and started following the sound. I lunged, targeting the smaller demon, the one with keys. He shouted, and I dodged as he swung his sword and then landed a strike on his ankle. He fell to the ground, and I seized the keys.

The other demon had figured out what I'd done and was racing back in my direction. I did not have long. The first key did not work on the door, and I had to stop my hand from trembling. Luckily, the second one turned. I flung open the door and slammed it shut behind me seconds before the other demon reached me.

As I leaned against the door, trying to catch a breath, I took in the dungeon in front of me. It was small, maybe ten cells total, five on each side. Most of them were empty. I ignored the urge to open the occupied ones. There would be time for that after Apep was destroyed, but that wouldn't happen without Shu.

I found Shu in the last cell on the left side. He looked tired and a bit rough for wear, but no visible scars or signs of injury, just as I had seen in my vision.

"Bastet, you made it!" Shu rushed to the bars.

"Of course I did, you think I'm going to let my only brother rot here?" I quickly spun the keys around, trying them on a steel door lock. I had no idea how long it would take the guards to break down the door.

The last key on the ring opened it, and Shu gave me a hug.

"I'm so sorry, sister."

"What? Why would you be apologizing to me?" I asked, confused.

"You are risking your life because I didn't see them coming. A child of Ra, captured by a group of common demons. I am ashamed. I am your elder brother. I should be protecting you, not the other way around."

I shook my head. "Shu, this is completely my fault. I let the prophecy fall into the wrong hands. Otherwise, he never would have baited me here, and—"

The door thrust open, and the guards rushed in. Shu responded immediately, releasing a large gust of wind from his hands that knocked the guards to the ground, the larger one dropping his sword in the process, which Shu quickly retrieved.

"We must keep moving! They might have called for backup." He gestured toward the door.

We sprinted down the hallway and ducked into a small storage room.

"Do you know where Apep is?" I whispered, as the visibility through the door was quite low, and it would be difficult to see if someone walked by. "Truth be told, I assumed he would be guarding you, since it's what he used to draw me here in the first place..."

"I actually haven't seen him," Shu said. "All I've seen are some guards. I knew about the deadline he gave you because they were talking about it."

"Hmm..." I consulted the all-seeing eye to get a grip on where else the action was. Sekhmet was still up top with the soldiers, fighting off the horde of demons. They were making some good headway at least.

Out of nowhere, one of the guards Shu had knocked over limped toward us. He threw his sword, which clearly had a poisoned tip, like how I had coated my daggers. It was going to hit me. I felt the same way I did at the lake with the crocodiles—time slowed down, even as I was actively deciding to dodge. I closed my eyes.

Time slowed. I tried to move—but Shu stepped in front of me, taking the blow in his shoulder.

"NO!" I yelled, panic filling me.

Shu collapsed to one knee, trying to stay upright. The demon guard had completely fallen. He had used the last of his energy to get his revenge and was either passed out or gone.

Shu sat down, holding on to his shoulder, bleeding profusely. He groaned in pain. "Demon blades are no joke…" His eyes started to glaze over.

"No, No, No, No," I repeated, beginning to rock back and forth as I held him. I needed to say something else, but it was the only sound I seemed capable of uttering. Should I take out the blade? That was what you were supposed to do, right? Or was that the wrong thing because then there was more bleeding?

I forced my body to stop rocking so I could figure out what to do, trying to fight off the panic.

It was rare for gods to bleed. Without poison or magical properties, the average god's skin would heal the moment the weapon left their skin.

If it hurt at all, it was usually a mere moment of discomfort.

I couldn't remember the last time I saw blood. I had forgotten how it had a smell, almost metallic. It overtook my senses.

Time was passing. Think, Bastet. Do something. I need to do something. I desperately wished someone else were here. My mother wouldn't be trapped in fear.

Thinking of her made me remember the bracelet. Shaking, I opened the ankh and took out the small vial of green liquid inside. The glow was comforting. "You're going to be okay," I promised him, my hand shaking as I forced open the lid.

"Save…that," he said, the words clearly taking effort.

"What are you talking about?" I demanded as I took off the lid. This was obviously the moment she had created this for.

"You…have no idea what else is going to happen tonight. You might need it…"

I suddenly had a memory of a time when I was a child. Shu was late to dinner, and most of the food was already gone. When I had offered him my last piece of bread, he refused, saying the same thing. To save it, because it was the Winter Solstice, and it would be a long and busy night.

I shook my head. My answer was going to be different than that night. "Don't be insane. I didn't come this far to let you die in an evil god's lair!"

His lips curved faintly, but he couldn't manage a full smile. "And they say Sekhmet is the stubborn one."

I yanked the blade out of his shoulder, and as I had expected, the blood gushed. My eyes went wide at the scene. I ripped off some fabric from my tunic and held it up to the bleeding, pushing down as hard as I could with my left hand, so I could use the dominant one to balance the vial.

Mother, if you can see us, please lend me your power. Your son deserves to live.

I poured it delicately. I could not mess this up. The liquid landed on the wound and began to spread out. The wound glowed, then faded—and so did the bleeding. Shu slumped against the wall, breathing easier.

I took a huge breath and leaned against the wall next to him. After a moment, the bleeding completely stopped, and I saw Shu visibly relax.

"Thank you for being stubborn," he joked.

I laughed, the kind that comes after shaken nerves. "I suppose it runs in the family. Are you still in any pain?"

He shook his head. "No, it feels as if nothing happened. Thank goodness for Mother leaving us some of her magic."

"I wonder if she expected me to use it so quickly," I pondered.

"I am sure she watches now, and is so proud of you, Bastet."

I blinked back tears. "Well, let's see if I actually succeed first."

I used the all-seeing eye to locate Sekhmet again so I could see the status of the fight again. Maybe they could help me search for Apep. It didn't seem like a good idea to go alone.

It made the most sense to rejoin them. I could tell my sister about the war room I had passed on the way to Shu.

But first, I checked for my father. I believed him to be true to his promise that he would "join at the right time". But after what had just happened to Shu, I wanted to see all my family safe. It would just take a moment to check on him.

Terror gripped my heart as I saw his location. I put my head in my hands. I didn't want to believe what I was seeing.

This can't be real.

"Sister, what is it?" Shu asked, noticing my expression change.

"It's father. I see him, and I see Apep… they're together. I don't understand, I thought he wanted to fight me, I don't…"

Suddenly, it all clicked. This was never about me, not really. Yes, Apep saw me as a threat because of the prophecy. But what threat could a young goddess be who didn't have her full powers? I wasn't the target, I was the same thing I had always been to him—an obstacle.

Distracted by saving Shu, he had finally gotten me out of the way, and there was nothing between himself and the god of the Sun.

I could tell from the images that they were in a throne room, as I could see the edges of a titanium chair that would certainly match that description.

"We have to go!" I yelled, throwing the door open. "I need you to get Sekhmet and tell her to meet me in the throne room of this lair!"

"What are you going to do?" I could tell he was hesitating, not wanting to leave me alone.
"I'm going to do my duty."

32

THE FACE OF CHAOS

There was no one in the halls as I ran, following the new pulsing light. Every footstep echoed off the empty walls, the sound unnerving in the silence.

I assumed that seeing Shu so close to death had sucked out all my energy, but adrenaline was coursing through me once again.

It all made sense now. Why did I run into so few obstacles freeing Shu? Had I truly believed they were keeping him outside the fray, or was my naivety simply on display again? It had seemed natural to me that Apep was with his forces, or hiding somewhere. But this had always been a trap—I had never questioned that.

I'd simply been wrong about who it was meant for.

How did I miss my dad leaving? How could he do this to us?

But I did not have time for answers. The light pulled me toward the room I had correctly assumed was the throne room earlier. The door stood wide open. I didn't hesitate, didn't stop to take a breath or prepare myself. I leaped through the entrance.

Apep was there.

He encircled the throne room in his massive, coiled serpent form. The sight sent a chill so deep through me that it almost stopped me in place. His black scales gleamed like obsidian, thick enough that no arrow or blade would pierce them. His eyes were pits of glowing red, his tongue—as long as my torso—flicked out, hissing. White fangs gleamed like polished bone.

My father was in the center of the ring the chaos god had created, holding a metal shield that covered nearly his full body in front of him. It glowed a light, delicate yellow.

I'm not too late!

"Daughter of Ra," he bellowed, his head spinning toward me. Those red eyes were now looking at me and the cold in the room deepened.

Keep it together. Keep it together. You are the daughter of Ra. It's you who Thoth made a prophecy about. Not Shu, not Sekhmet, not one of the war gods fighting up on deck. It has to be you.

"Bastet, GET BEHIND ME!" my father bellowed.

Apep's tail swung toward me.

I had no time to plan, to feel fear, to do anything but jump.

Without my feline reflexes, I may not have made the landing, but my feet hit the floor without stumbling and dashed behind my father's shield.

I placed my hand on my chest. I made it.

"What are you doing?" my father demanded, briefly taking his eyes off the chaos god. His voice was strained from the effort of holding up our defense.

I ignored the pounding of my heart and drew out my daggers, standing up tall. "I saved Shu…"

The words came out too soft, betraying my fear. I pushed my chest out, aimed my daggers high, and tried again. "And now I'm here to end this." I swung my body around to face Apep and held his gaze.

I didn't believe that—not fully. My goal was to stall, to buy Sekhmet and the others enough time to arrive. Shu would be getting them as quickly as he could.

Apep laughed, a sound empty of any joy. "You are foolish. But that is why you fell for my gambit."

I shrugged. "Fell for it? I was always going to fight you; you simply sped up the process." I tried to think of something Sekhmet might say. "Really, I should be thanking you." I forced a casual smirk.

"Not only foolish," he hissed. "You're also arrogant. Truly, your father's daughter." He turned to my father, who was still looking at me.

His voice sounded more strained than before as he said, "Bastet, you must go. This has always been between me and him. Please."

I locked eyes with him. I had trouble reading his face, but I did not see fear, or sadness, just iron resolve.

"What are you doing here?" My voice broke, my confidence slipping away. "You said you'd join the fight when the time is right, not offer yourself up to the enemy!"

"Daughter, I did not lie to you. This is the right time. The time that I could ensure my children were still safe. I'm what he wants." He glanced at Apep, daring him to disagree with his words.

I was confused why the evil god had not yet attacked him. My father's shield, and whatever light powers it contained, had to be weak here so far from the sun. But clearly it was working, as we were both still alive.

I needed to know why. I needed the full picture.

"What are you waiting for then?" I taunted Apep, channeling my sister again. "Why haven't you struck?"

"Because your father has invoked an ancient, ridiculous magical loophole," the chaos god hissed. "He is answering the prayers of his people for his safety. Their words power his shield. Amun will not stop a god from answering a noble prayer."

Relief washed through me—Father wasn't simply lying down to die. His words before the battle, telling me I would be his successor, and the look on his face when I entered… I had been afraid he had accepted death.

He must have instructed his priests to ask the mortals for extra prayers. I had always thought about what we could offer them; I had never realized they could also protect us.

If I make it out of here alive, I promise to do right by you, people of Egypt.

"But they will not last forever," Apep continued. "Even the god of the sun will run out of ka at some point. We are far from his precious light."

Dread gripped me. We were running out of time. Had Shu made it to the deck yet? Was the skirmish up there even done?

Either way, I still had to stall. Shu's political lessons, I had always been advised that one thing confident gods loved to do was talk. And you needed confidence to take on Ra, even here, on your own ground.

I was in a stalemate. The very thing the three of us lived with for so long.

The last one.

"What is your obsession with my father anyway? You control all this," I motioned around me to represent his lair and territory of Duat as a whole. "You are more powerful than most gods could dream of—you literally put the world into darkness and let it sleep every night."

"All this?" He turned his head toward me, away from my father. Good. My bait was working.

I exaggerated my gestures. "Yes, do you not also nearly have a hundred soldiers and a plethora of lower gods under your command? Some would kill for less." I tried to pick my words carefully, lest anything I say cross the line from distracting to infuriating enough to attack me, shield or not.

"You insolent child," he snarled. "You understand NOTHING! I was stripped of my power the moment Amun introduced order into this forsaken world. Before there was light and dark, there was only unity, chaos, existence without the need for control and rules. There was freedom."

"So that's your goal?" I edged a little closer to the door, just in case. "Destroy any semblance of harmony and structure?"

"Did you not hear me?" He flung his tail around. "There was harmony when there was no 'structure' that you speak of. Gods could be themselves. There were no mortals we had to answer to. We simply lived as we pleased, and no one was above anyone else."

It was strange to imagine a world with no mortals. I could not fathom powers with no purpose, gods wandering through eternity with nothing to do. Was that his plan? To get rid of mortals if he took my father's power? I shivered involuntarily.

But I guessed it was about more than just a desire to live in leisure or achieve some kind of purely democratic society. That wasn't enough to explain all of this. "What you mean is no one was above you," I theorized. "When my father came to be, you became just another god under Amun."

"Just another god," he scoffed. "He has treated me as a misfit child, trapped in this prison!" I could tell he was growing tired of my talking, as his eyes were not staying locked on me anymore, but switching between me and my father.

The light around my father's shield was beginning to dim, and my breath caught in my throat.

We're out of time.

I considered raising my own feeble shield— even for a moment's protection—but I had no access to light, no prayers to call on.

Then, suddenly, the doors burst open. Sekhmet, Shu, and the rest of the battalion stormed in with a battle cry. Shu slammed the doors shut with a gust of wind. Horus leapt to the front, brandishing a massive spear that made mine look like a child's toy.

Sekhmet had trained her troops well. They did not mimic the failed efforts of those whom I had read about in the library. No one tried to cut off Apep's tail. There was no stabbing or swinging of swords just yet.

Instead, they moved in perfect unison, jumping on top of him.

They're trying to hold him down.

They weren't fighting him…they were preparing the way for me.

I saw Henet running toward his tail, and I opened my mouth to warn her, to tell her not to go alone.

But before she even made it within a foot, Apep flicked it and hurled her against the wall. She crumpled to the ground. The sound overpowered all the others. I ran to her side, showing anyone in my way. Time stopped. Had I been struck, too? My heart was certainly aching.

"Henet, Henet!" I yelled, kneeling beside her.

Her hair was stained with blood. A mortal blow like this would not have fazed her. But Apep's tail had speed and strength that was unmatched. I pressed my ear to her chest, listening desperately for a heartbeat; it was there, but slow.

She's still alive, I've got to do something. I saved Shu; I can save her.

"B…B…stet…" she croaked, her voice ragged.

"Where is a healer?" I demanded, glancing behind me.

Shu walked up to me and gently put his hand on my shoulder. "Sister…"

"Where. Is A. Healer?" I demanded again, putting emphasis on each word.

Henet shakily grabbed my hand. "Bastet, it's too late."

I shook my head, tears stinging my eyes. "Of course it's not. We did find one of those, right?" I looked for Sekhmet. Where is she? We could use her bracelet!

"She got severely injured in the spar up above," Shu explained to me. "She didn't come down here with us."

Blood was soaking through my shirt. I hated the smell—thick, metallic. "No, No…there has to be something… WHERE IS SEKHMET?"

"Sister, Sekhmet gave that healer her potion, so she could rest up and be ready to take care of the wounded after the fight."

My whole body was shaking.

"Bastet, it's okay," Henet said, her voice a little stronger but still strained. "It has been an honor to serve you; it always has."

I shook my head. "Don't say that! You are no soldier, no servant! You are my friend! One of my only friends in my small, pitiful excuse for a life!"

She smiled faintly. "And your life will not be small anymore, Bastet. Look around you; we are all here to end this. You and Sekhmet will be free, and you will be a wonderful god."

The tears blurred my vision. "I didn't want anyone to die. I'd stay on that boat forever if it meant…"

She shushed me gently. "I have no regrets. I do not wish you to have them either. Should you someday meet an untimely demise, we will hopefully be reunited in the fields of the gods. If not, it means you are living the full and wonderful life you deserve."

I had no words, my breath hitched, and the tears escalated to full sobs.

"Can you promise me something?" she asked.

I wiped my left eye and forced myself to speak. "Any-any-thing Henet, anything at all."

"Would you ask Thoth to note my name in the record of this fight?"

"What?" It was the last thing I expected her to ask.

"I want my family to read that I went out valiantly, with glory. They might not believe it if it comes from my best friend, but they will believe it if it comes from the god of knowledge." Her voice was so quiet now that it was almost a whisper. "Perhaps…it will…ease their suffering, to know I died for a reason."

Her poor parents. How could I ever look them in the eye again?

"I will make sure you have your own dedicated page," I promised.

And then her eyes closed.

33

THE FINAL STAND

It was unfathomable. I knew people died in war. There was no question Apep was a force of evil. But somewhere in my mind, I thought if anyone died, it would be me. Was that just arrogance? After saving Shu, had I thought we were invincible?

I had forgotten Shu was still behind me. "Sister, we must get back to the fight. They can't hold him forever."

I shook my head. "I'm a useless fighter. What can I do?" I picked my daggers from where I had placed them next to Henet. "Take these, you or Sekhmet can finish this. I'm sure you have better aim."

He grabbed my arm. "Bastet, I am sorry for your loss, really, I am. But do you want her sacrifice to mean nothing?"

"Of course not," I snapped, yanking my arm away.

"Then you have to go back in there and finish this. No one else can do this."

Of course he was right; I had repeated the same thing to myself when I entered the room. But it was hard to believe now, after watching death take someone I loved.

But I remembered what I had told Keket about the prophecy and our destiny. That if we couldn't believe in ourselves, we had to believe in the power of words.

I don't have to believe in myself. I only needed to trust my destiny.

He helped me to my feet, and I allowed myself one more moment of grief. And then I gripped the daggers and followed him back into the fray.

Shu was right; they had him pinned down, using a lot of effort. All the major gods were focused on holding Apep down, while some of the lower gods were fighting off enemy guards that had followed them down. My father had taken Henet's place and was holding down the tail.

"Bastet, now!" Sekhmet yelled. She was tying Apep's mouth together, straining with the effort.

I ran over the top of his head and jumped on the scales. I would only be able to get the right angle from above his face. I raised my daggers high, summoning all my strength. "This is for Henet!" I yelled.

But as I brought the blades down, Apep vanished from my sight. Panic gripped me. How could he still escape, even bound?

My brain was suddenly overtaken by visions. I saw Sekhmet and Shu lying on the ground like Henet, eyes lifeless. Ptah, at my funeral, tears in his eyes. The sky is turning red before falling into endless darkness.

No. I could not let these thoughts take hold. I needed my mind to be clear.

I took a deep breath, focusing on one thing alone—the face of the chaos god. If I could not see him with my natural eyes, I would have to use the other. I poured all of my thoughts into it, sacrificing every other sense.

But I had never been able to use my powers for anything but finding those I loved. And I had no love for Apep; how would I do this? I tried to summon hate—and though I felt it, it was tangled with grief.

Everyone I had been able to see before was because of either blood or an emotional connection. Although it made me sick to my stomach, I tried to pin down the exact emotion I felt for Apep. Just like me, he was trapped in an unfulfilled life. He was not free. He was not with his children.

I did not feel sympathy for him. He thrived on death and chaos. But I did feel a strong sense of pity for him—the kind you feel for a pathetic creature. He had no one to love, no real power, nothing good to anchor him.

I let that feeling of pity fill me. I did not think of anyone else, only a sad, despicable god alone in a corner. A god that needed to die.

Suddenly, his image flared in my mind, inches behind me. I spun and drove both daggers into his eye, striking with a precision I didn't expect. A surge of magical force blasted me backward. I hit the ground hard, my arm stinging.

A bellow tore from Apep's throat; a sound of a hiss and growl combined. When his head began to convulse, it was clear we had won.

His death was not quick. I turned away when I was sure he would not rise again. The sight was too much to bear.

When the room was still, the gods slowly stood. Some had been kicked aside by Apep's final thrash, but everyone was alive.

I ran over to my siblings, who were standing in the corner. Shu looked fine, Sekhmet had a scratch, but nothing was too concerning. "Where is Father?" I asked, my eyes darting around the room.

Shu gestured toward the door, where I saw him leaning against Horus. "We forced him to go upstairs; He was about to pass out."

Is it truly over?

Before I could check on anyone else, Anubis appeared through the fog.

The jackal-headed death god only came in person for the death of a god. It was never handled the same. Sometimes justice had to be rendered. Killing another god was highly forbidden.

Like a mortal, he even judged the soul of a deity. No one living other than Anubis himself had seen what the next plane looked like for an immortal.

He surveyed the scene. "You have killed the god of chaos."

Someone must explain. I desperately wished my father were there to speak for us.

Using whatever energy I had left, I stepped forward. "I am sure you can understand the justification of this death."

He cut me off. "Do not worry, Bastet. You do not need to explain or defend yourself. Apep has long brought misery to this plane. If I could have done it myself, I would have—but it could only be you."

I breathed a sigh of relief, and with it, the last bits of adrenaline in my veins left. My body felt heavy.

"Where will you take him?" Sekhmet asked.

I did not expect him to answer, but he did. "This is a being who no longer needs to exist in any world or reality. I will give his soul to Amitt, and he will cease to exist."

What a strange concept to wrap my head around. Death was something I could picture. I had seen it almost every day in Duat. I came face to face with it today, and saw the light leave Henet's eyes.

I even understood reincarnation, the gift given to those most loyal to the gods. Was it a fate worse than death? If so, Apep deserved it.

Anubis's golden scales appeared above Apep's lifeless body. It was likely performative, as his fate had already been decided. The feather representing goodness was on the left, and Apep's soul—a dark, bleak-looking thing—was on the right. It sank immediately, and Anubis nodded.

He raised his staff, a mix of gold and black onyx with a forked end, and placed it on Apep's head. Slowly, the body began to dissolve. Within a minute, it was gone—only a few scales and blood remained.

Anubis met my gaze, then turned to my sister. "Daughters of Ra, you have earned your freedom. I hope you never have to see me again." He nodded as a final sign of farewell and vanished back into the mist.

I glanced over at Sekhmet. "What do you think happens now?"

She grinned. "I have not the faintest idea, sister—but aren't you excited to find out?"

34

THE APPROACHING DAWN

We arrived back at the ship minutes before dawn. The mood of the group was strange—we were victorious, but also fewer in number than when we had left. Henet was the only casualty I was connected to, but some of Sekhmet's soldiers had passed as well. Many more were injured, though now we could finally get them to a healer god.

The entire ride was a blur, my eyes fluttering open and closed as I fought sleep.

My father told us that until Amun laid his blessing upon us, our restrictions were not lifted. "I wish I could free you at this exact moment," he said. "I hardly have words to show my appreciation for what you two have done today—not just for your family, but for all the gods and people of Egypt. I just ask you to wait a little bit longer."

I wasn't sure about Sekhmet, but I honestly didn't care. My body and mind were yearning to rest anyway. Plus, the idea of talking to anyone, even my family or Ptah, sounded exhausting. Even if we had our freedom, I would have chosen sleep anyway.

This was not the first dawn I had wished away. I could miss one more.

After passing out in the cabin, I had strange dreams. They were short, fragmented, and shifted quickly. In one, I was riding through Duat in the Meneset when suddenly the sky blazed bright, blinding the normal stars. The sea below me turned to sand, and there was nowhere left for the ship to go.

When I woke up, I was back in my room. It was well past twilight. When I saw the time on the sundial, my first instinct was to jump up as if it were any other night. I'm late! I must get to the ship!

"You don't have to worry about that anymore," a voice said.

I looked up to see Ptah leaning against the door. "Apologies, I hope it is not disconcerting that I have been here, I just knew you would wake up soon..." He stepped closer. "I had to actually see with my own eyes that you were unharmed."

"It's alright!" I insisted, trying to sit up. I was so happy to see him. But my muscles protested, and I sank back down. My arm ached; that bruise would be nasty. Ptah grabbed my desk chair and sat beside me. He held out his hand, and I grabbed it. It was so nice to feel the warmth.

"Your father is making the journey through Duat alone tonight," he explained. "There is no danger."

I had never asked him what would happen to the sun when we were finally free. Strange, that I had not thought of the very thing that I was dictated to my whole life. "No one will guard it anymore?"

"Ra himself won't even carry it after tonight; it will likely be delegated to half-gods from now on. Just like you, your father will be free."

I wondered what he would do with it.

What am I going to do with it?

I wasn't in Duat tonight because of defiance or preparation for battle. I just…didn't need to be there. It was surreal. The thought was almost disorienting.

I thought about the conversation with my sister when we went to find our aunt. Even then, with the battle so close, it still felt hypothetical. A nice idea, something to dream about, but not real.

Not until now.

"Now that you're awake, would you like to make up our date tonight?" Ptah asked, gently squeezing my hand. "That is, if you don't need to rest more…"

I smiled. "That sounds wonderful. But I want to be fully present for that. I don't think I can offer you that right now. Plus…there is something I need to do first. Is that alright?"

"Of course it is, I just—"

He brushed a hand across my forehead. "Bastet, I'm just glad you're alright. If something had happened to you…"

I forced myself to sit up straighter so I could meet his gaze. "I was always going to come back to you."

I made my way to Thoth's temple. It was not the day of his public audience, but hopefully, he would see me regardless. I took my time walking through Heliopolis, adjusting to this strange new freedom. It was strange, not having this internal timer driving my every move. If I wanted, I could stay out all night, wandering around the city—and when dawn began to arrive, nothing would happen.

I felt a twinge of nervousness when speaking to an attendant, remembering what had happened last time. But I reminded myself that the risk was minimal now; Thoth had surely rooted out any remaining spies after I had exposed the last one.

Still, I sought out a priest whom I recognized from the public audience. "Bastet, the daughter of Ra, would like to inquire about a private meeting."

He nodded. "He has anticipated your arrival. Please follow me to his private office."

Of course, he had. I should have guessed. What must it be like to always see what was coming? I'm not sure I would like it. Life needed some mystery.

The priest led me to a small office on the opposite side of the temple, before bowing and walking away. The space could not have been more different from Thoth's throne room. Instead of a grand, almost imposing environment, the office felt like a library. Here, parchment covered every wall and surface.

Thoth looked up and smiled as I entered. "Bastet, I hear that congratulations are in order."

"Thank you," I responded. "Though truthfully, it feels as if my contributions were the smallest factor in our victory."

"That's not what your father told me this morning," Thoth said, smiling. "But your humility is admirable."

"My father came to see you today?" A lot must have happened while I was out.

"Yes, a few have been here to see me—to attempt and get a new look at their future, now that the god of chaos is gone."

"Ah, yes," I replied, suddenly feeling embarrassed. "Speaking of messages of the future, I wanted to apologize for letting your prophecy about me fall into the wrong hands. I assure you, it was the last thing I wanted."

To my relief, I detected no anger in Thoth's voice. "It is not a situation I wish like to see repeated," he said. "But in this case, it hastened your destiny and ended up being a part of the story."

"You'll be recording all this, right?" I asked, remembering my reason for coming over.

"Yes, this fight deserves a mention in the history of our world."

"And you'll write about…everyone?" I thought of the battles and records I read through in preparation for fighting Apep. While some were quite detailed, others focused on a few people who were key to achieving victory. There may have been mentions of the number of soldiers, but some didn't even get named.

"I will write about those that are necessary to preserve the story," Thoth replied. "What is it you truly wish to ask, daughter of Ra?"

"I need you to write about Henet," I exclaimed. For a moment, the image of her crumpled body on the floor flashed in my mind, but I pushed it away. That's not how I would remember her.

"She was one of the soldiers in this fight. She died in the final face-off with Apep. She gave her life to ensure Sekhmet, and I could have ours. She fought bravely to help us protect the sun, and she deserves to be remembered."

Thoth nodded slowly. "Tell me more about her."

And so I did, about her humor, her companionship, her loyalty, and her bravery. About how she had a promising future ahead of her, as an up-and-coming goddess. And how she sacrificed it all without any bitterness.

Thoth wrote down notes as I spoke. I was grateful he took my request seriously. "Alright, Bastet, her story will be included. I can see she was a great friend and fought with honor."

"Thank you," I turned to leave, grateful he had been convinced without much effort.

"Do you have any opinions on your own portrayal?" he asked, stopping me.

I shook my head. "I will let my actions speak for me."

Feeling lighter now with my promise to Henet fulfilled, I returned to Ra's temple, where Ptah awaited me with dinner. It was just as beautiful a meal as the last one. I realized I was ravenous; I had not eaten since before the battle.

We kept the conversation light, which I was grateful for. There would be a time I would want to unpack the emotions of that night. But not tonight.

Instead, we looked to the future. We talked about all the things we wanted to do together now that I could be in the sun—spend time on the beach, paint the creatures of the sea, and we could even leave Heliopolis! I had never seen another city, let alone the countryside of Egypt.

We were eating dessert when Sekhmet popped in.

"Apologies for the interruption," she said. "But I have come with news. Sister, you and I are to see Amun in the morning, to receive our blessing."

My heart leapt. Father had not given us a time we could meet with the king of the gods. But now—by this time tomorrow—our new lives would truly begin. The life I was just planning with Ptah.

"One more day," I said to her.

She smiled. "Just one more."

35

THE LIGHT OF THE DAY

The next morning had arrived. We were meeting with Amun right before dawn. Even though I knew it wouldn't, I couldn't help but picture suddenly falling asleep in front of not only him but any onlookers, falling to the ground.

I had not realized there would be an audience until we arrived, which made me grateful for carefully choosing an outfit worthy of meeting the king of the gods. I wore my nicest dress, made of white silk, and had even put on a bit of makeup.

My sister, who had shown few signs of anxiety leading up to or during our big fight, was suddenly holding my hand as we approached the stage. Leave it to her to fear authority more than any enemy.

The stage in the center of the town was gilded, like many royal things. When not in use for a ceremony, it was usually used by street performers or vendors. Sometimes, during holidays or large festivals, it would be decorated in honor of the occasion. I had never had reason to stand upon it before.

The crowd below was a large one. I saw the expected faces—our father, Hathor, and Shu—I was grateful to see Ptah near the front. I gave him a small wave. Unsurprisingly for my sister, Montu was present as well.

But what I hadn't expected was that nearly everyone who had fought with us was watching. I recognized some of the soldiers and even the recruited gods like Horus and Anuket. Many faces I didn't recognize were present, too.

It made me self-conscious, suddenly checking to make sure my dress didn't have any creases or stains or something. I had never stood in front of this many people before.

But I suppose I, too, would want to see the crowning of new gods.

Amun was everything you'd expect from the king of the gods. It was impossible not to look at him. His skin was blue, a color reserved for him alone, and seemed to almost glitter in the sun. It was said his head could take the shape of any animal he desired. Currently, it is in the form of a ram.

Upon his head was a tall crown, made of titanium that was anodized and changed colors as he moved. Diamonds outlined the bottom and the top edges of the band, but what was more impressive was the sheer variety of stones that filled up the rest of it—rubies, lapis lazuli, amethysts, and some I didn't even recognize. And yet, it all looked cohesive.

Amun approached us, stopping a couple of feet ahead. He briefly addressed the crowd below us. "On this day, we come together to celebrate the efforts of the daughters of Ra. While I do not interfere with many of the matters of gods, I do not pretend that I was not hoping for their success. The god of Egypt owes you a debt for freeing us from chaos."

A part of me wanted to pipe up and say it was our duty, or admit that I did it for myself more than anyone else, but I stayed quiet.

"Please kneel," he directed.

I shot Sekhmet a look, unsure what was happening, but she just nodded.

After we had complied, he lifted his scepter and touched it to the top of our heads, starting with mine and then moving to Sekhmet's.

"In reward for your services, I award you with full god-hood. You are also freed from your restrictions and may choose when you sleep or awaken."

Just as he said the words, I felt sunlight touch my skin. It was dawn. And I was awake.

Then I experienced what could only be described as the warmth of light fill me. All the fatigue and soreness from the fight left my body. I stretched out my hands and felt newfound strength. My mind felt sharper. It was all natural, as if there had been a dam within me holding back water, releasing what had always been waiting.

I was not sure what I was capable of yet, which was kind of exciting. I wanted to run off to a field somewhere and lift my hands, just to see if light would shoot out or not. I wanted to feel the sun against my skin.

I did not expect him to continue. "Additionally, to your awakening to your true selves, I will also grant you one wish each—a reward. Although, as I am sure you can understand, I retain the right to accept or refuse."

A wish? Has this happened before? I searched my mind for the stories of heroes of the past. A part of me vaguely remembered something, but not what the hero had asked for. Still, we stopped the world from being plunged into eternal darkness. I suppose that warranted something.

I looked toward Sekhmet, who seemed to be thinking deeply. I decided to go first.

"I want my own festival," I blurted out. It was the first thing that came to mind, but as I explained it, it felt right, even though my sister had her eyebrow raised. "A Feast of Bubastis. Held in the section of the Nile near my temple. To make up for the years I received prayers without answers, I want to be able to answer one significant request on that day without using any of my ka."

My power would already be strongest on a festival day, so I understood my request was not a small one. When my request was done, I stopped talking and watched Amun nervously for his response.

"I have no issues providing you with a festival," he said. "However, to grant you the freedom to grant a prayer with no associated cost of ka…" He paused.

"Alright," he finally agreed. "I will allow you this power. But the request must align with what is good for the Egyptian people. Should you grant something that brings harm to any of our worshippers, I will intervene. Is that understood?"

I nodded and bowed. "Thank you." I wondered if Hathor would help me plan. The visions I had from my childhood returned to me —cats in gold and dancing women—and they no longer seemed so silly now. I hoped that the girl would be proud of me today. That we used our wish to do good for our people.

"Sekhmet, what do you wish for?" Amun asked, moving on from me.

She stepped forward, slowly, almost tripping. I had never seen her so nervous.

"I wish for healing powers, like my mother."

"Very well," he said, looking relieved that her request was simple. He leaned his staff against her head, and she glowed faintly, like when our powers had first been unlocked.

I was surprised by her answer. I am not sure what I had expected, maybe some kind of weapon or advantage over her enemies? But it was touching to see her honor our mother this way. I personally had no wish to see injuries or be in places where such powers were needed, but I felt great respect for what our mother did, especially since her vial had saved Shu's life.

He returned to the crowd. "Now, please go and enjoy this day of celebration. This is the beginning of your burgeoning service as full deities. Your life will soon change. Take this moment to appreciate the challenges you have overcome to get here." The audience clapped.

We stepped off the stage, where our father was waiting for us. He took us both in a huge hug, the first we had received since we were quite young children. We exchanged surprised looks.

He stopped quickly, lest anyone see this overt sign of affection not commonly seen by the ancient gods.

"I am so proud of you both," he said upon releasing us. "I knew this day would come…"

He clearly saw my crossed arms and laughed, correcting himself. "I hoped this day would come. I know you are both capable of great things. The people of Egypt will greatly benefit from your ascension."

"I may still seek your consultation upon occasion," Sekhmet said, almost nervously. "I may miss the war room when I'm gone."

This was as close as she had come to admitting she would miss living in Ra's temple.

My father smiled. "My temple will always be your home," he promised, looking at us both.

"Even if Hathor and you have more children?" Sekhmet questioned.

I couldn't pretend the idea hadn't crossed my mind, but as always, her candor took me back. Especially during such a nice moment.

He did not look offended. "Your rooms will always be open," he promised. "Hathor wouldn't have it any other way. I wish you'd give her more of a chance, daughter…"

I expected her to snap back, say something sarcastic, but she only nodded. "Hathor, perhaps we should go out to lunch one of these days."

Lunch, what a novel idea. I had to stop myself from giggling.

Before Hathor could reply, Shu walked up to us, holding hands with Tefnut. "Well, if it isn't my sisters getting their own wishes granted by Amun.

But no special treatment for the god trapped in the underwater dungeon, eh?" he joked.

"Well, don't give up quite yet, perhaps the next time you get captured by a dark deity, you'll get your own festival," I responded, laughing. In truth, I did think he deserved some kind of assurance. Without him, I would never have been able to find Apep. But he would never accept it.

"I've got everything I need right here," he said, squeezing Tefnut's hand. "Speaking of which, I believe Ptah is looking for you."

My heart sped up. I had seen he was somewhere in the crowd, as I checked once we stepped on stage. But I had been so distracted talking to my family, I hadn't kept an eye on his whereabouts. I quickly sensed he was at the edge of the crowd, on the other side of the city square. "I'm going to him," I told everyone.

No one was surprised, and I took my exit.

I closed my eyes and located Ptah—he was sitting on a bench just outside the square, at a crossroads by the street where our temples reside.

I did not want to push myself through the crowd and risk someone trying to stop and talk to me, so I slunk behind a building to take the long way around.

But I still ran into someone.

It was Keket.

It was strange to see her out in the open. She carried herself differently, dressed in a sparkling black dress with stars.

"Bastet, I was hoping to catch you…"

I smiled. "Looks like you did."

"Congratulations on your ascension, and your victory, I suppose…" She returned my smile, sheepishly.

It was strange to meet her in a different emotional setting. There was no impending danger over our heads; I wasn't on guard and searching for double meanings in everything she said.

"Congratulations on your ascension and getting out of that cave," I joked.

Her smile dropped. "I feel…Guilty, I was not there with you during the fight."

I wasn't expecting that. "No, that's not what I meant. It isn't your fault your father cursed the entrance."

"Yes, but…" she replied slowly, "I am not sure if I would have joined you anyway. I believe I was too afraid." She bit her lip.

I chose my words carefully. "There is no need to look back," I told her. "The important thing is, you're stepping into your role as god of the stars, right?"

As I expected, her eyes lit up. "Yes. I was terrified no one would want to work with me because of who my father was. But they've all been really welcoming. Including your father."

"He understands how important you are to maintaining peace in Duat."

"You're lucky to have him," she replied softly. "It's why you've turned out so brave and good. Do you think…there's any chance for me, based on who mine was?"

"My father didn't want me to do any of this," I pointed out. "And while that wasn't for any kind of notorious reason, I did this because it was what I wanted. Because I wanted more for me, my sister, and even for you. The point is…Keket, you can be whoever you'd like."

She smiled again at that.

"And besides," I continued, "Your mother is one of the bravest people I've ever met. She came to meet me, risking everything, because she wanted to protect you above all else.

"You're right," she said. "I hope we can be friends now."

"Yes, that would be nice."

Even now, I feel a connection between us, the daughters of prophecy, now stepping up into our new roles.

I remembered Ptah was waiting for me. "See you later, Keket!"

Ptah was sitting on a bench near the street corner leading to Bubastis. He stood up when I approached. "Oh Bast…"

We closed the gap between us and ran into each other's arms. The kiss this time felt like a celebration—so different from the night in his room, where I worried it might be our last. This felt like the beginning of forever.

He grabbed my hand. "I have to show you something."

We walked to my temple. I realized I was going to be living there now as we approached. I had barely even seen the living quarters since we designed them. I'm sure Pawarem kept them clean, but it would be odd to sleep alone.

He took me inside. The cats were active today; there must be a dozen more since my last visit. They all seemed grateful to see me. Remembering I had access to my true powers, I closed my eyes and conjured a pile of fish in the center of the floor. They all ran to it in a clamor.

Ptah laughed. "I should've expected that was the first thing you'd use your powers on."

I shrugged. "Well it's obviously important to do a test run." It felt electrifying to see how much *ka* I had now. Normally, I never would have wasted magic on something so frivolous.

"Only makes me feel better about my gift," he said, tugging me upstairs.

I was right, the living quarters were well-maintained in my absence. I noticed someone, likely Pawarem, had hung up some of our paintings on the walls. That was a nice touch. Each one was tied to a great memory. A perfect place to make more.

I noticed a door leading to a balcony on the left side. "Has that always been here?" I asked.

Ptah raised an eyebrow. "You really haven't been here in a long time, have you?" He opened the door and led me outside.

The balcony was beautiful—spotless marble with a glass roof, so no brightness was kept from shining in. It was perfectly positioned to receive the maximum amount of sunlight. On top of that, it was a safe space to host some cats, who lounged in a chair in the corner.

"You made this, didn't you?" I realized. I sat down on the plush lounge chair to experience the true weight of it all.

"Yes," he said sheepishly. "I couldn't focus on anything once you left my room that night. I hated that you were in danger. I had to distract myself somehow. Additionally, I knew you needed a place like this in your temple. A place to revel in the light."

I kissed him again, light and fast. "Thank you. This will be a great place for us both." I could picture us here, welcoming the sunrise, for years to come. In fact, it was difficult to imagine my future in this place without seeing him in every room. It was all open to us now, the world of possibilities.

"Both?" he asked.

I blushed. "Well, I mean, like eventually, someday when…"

He grabbed my hand, smiling. "What makes you think I would be the one to leave my temple?" he teased me.

I panicked for a moment, but he noticed and quickly continued. "I jest, Bast. I would never take all of this from you. You earned it."

I leaned my head on his shoulder. "Thank you. For the daggers, for this temple, for the balcony, for…everything."

He squeezed my hand. "You're welcome."

Amun had been right—this was the start of a new life, full of responsibilities, trials, and perhaps more battles to fight. But for as long as I could, I wanted to live in this moment. As a goddess with the whole world ahead of me, a boy I loved on my side, and the sun touching my face. I never had to miss this again.

"You want to hear what I think?" he asked.

"Yes?"

"I think you are a cat who is going to thrive in the light of the day."

ACKNOWLEDGEMENTS

The dream of finishing and releasing a novel into the world is a dream I have had for around two decades now, and it could not have happened by my hand alone.

I would like to express my appreciation to the following people:

My fantastic cover artist K. Jaspersen, who helped me bring my vision to life. Victoria of Victoria Jane Editorial, whose developmental edits made me a better writer. Finally, MavenThoria and Emilie Mortati helped get this manuscript in an acceptable place to actually be ready with their copy editing/proofing efforts.

In closing, I want to thank those in my personal life who got me to this point. To my husband, for believing in my dream during a time it was not convenient for me to write a book, and to my parents for teaching me how to believe in my potential and who shared with me their appreciation for the written word.

ABOUT THE AUTHOR

Miranda was one credit shy of a Creative Writing minor, and is still slightly bitter about it— but fan fiction was also a fantastic teacher. She lives in Tennessee with her husband, a cat, and a dog.

You can learn more about her and her writing at https://mirandalenwest.com